County Corr. Road Runners

By

Matthew Colfer
@matthewcolfer2023

Terms and Conditions
LEGAL NOTICE

© Copyright 2023 ©**matthewcolfer**

All rights reserved. The content contained within this book may not be reproduced, duplicated, or transmitted without direct written permission from the author or the publisher. Email requests to kevin@babystepspublishing.com

Under no circumstances will any blame or legal responsibility be held against the publisher, or author, for any damages, reparation, or monetary loss due to the information contained within this book, either directly or indirectly.

Legal Notice:

This book is copyright protected. It is only for personal use. You cannot amend, distribute, sell, use, quote, or paraphrase any part, or the content within this book, without the consent of the author or publisher.

Disclaimer Notice:

Please note the information contained within this document is for educational and entertainment purposes only. All effort has been executed to present accurate, up-to-date, reliable, complete information. No warranties of any kind are declared or implied. Readers acknowledge the author is not engaging in the rendering of legal, financial, medical, or professional advice. The content within this book has been derived from various sources. Please consult a licensed professional before attempting any techniques outlined in this book.

By reading this document, the reader agrees under no circumstances is the author responsible for any losses, direct or indirect, that are incurred as a result of the use of the information contained within this document, including, but not limited to, errors, omissions, or inaccuracies.

Published by Babysteps Publishing Limited All enquires to kevin@babystepspublishing.com

ISBN- 9798872260509

Table of Contents

County Con: Road Runners 1
Chapter 1: DUI (Drinking Under the Influence) 3
Chapter 2: Another Day in Milford 13
   The Next Day: Milford, Afternoon, 12:00 PM 13
Chapter 3: The Empty Safe 25
   Todd Hunter's House: Afternoon 12:30 pm 25
   Old Man Wilson's Property: Afternoon 1:00 pm 30
   Somewhere in the Pike County Wilderness 33
Chapter 4: Guardian Angel 39
   Shaw's Bar, Evening: 7:00 pm 39
   Tracy Kean's House: Evening 7:15 pm 52
   Milford Sheriff's Department: Evening 9:00 pm 56
Chapter 5: Runaway 59
   Jim Gold's House: Evening 9:10 pm 59
   Tracy Kean's House: Evening 10:05 pm 61
   Downtown Milford: Evening 10:15 pm 64
   The Back Roads of Pike County, Evening 10:25 pm 66
Chapter 6: Last Seen Alive 71
   Jim Gold's House: Evening 11:15 pm 71
   The Back Roads of Pike County: 11:21 pm 72
   Jim Gold's House: Morning 7:00 am 74
   Tracy Kean's House: Morning 7:07 am 75
Chapter 7: The Investigation Begins 83

Milford Sheriff's Department: Morning, 8:09 am 83
1 Hour Later 86
Somewhere in the Pike County Wilderness 87

Chapter 8: Deep Pains 93
Milford Sheriff's Department: Morning 10:15 am 93
Tracy Kean's House: Morning 10:30 am 105

Chapter 9: Uninvited Guests 109
Milford Sheriff's Department: Morning 10:40 am 109
Somewhere in the Pike County Wilderness 114

Chapter 10: Initiative and Deceit 119
Shaw's Bar, Evening 10:30 pm 119
Johnson Residence, the next morning 9:30 am 123
Milford Diner, Morning 10:00 am 129

Chapter 11: A Dark Discovery 135
Milford Sheriff's Department: Morning 10:30 am 135
The Back Roads of Pike County, Morning 11:00 am 136
The Back Roads of Pike County, Morning 11:35 am 139
Johnson Residence, Afternoon 12:05 pm 141

Chapter 12: The Search for Clues 143
Milford Clinic, Afternoon 12:10 pm 143
Milford Sheriff's Department, Afternoon 12:20 pm 144
Milford Sheriff's Department, Afternoon 12:30 pm 146
Temporary FBI Office, Afternoon 12:49 149

Chapter 13: Hostage Negotiations 153
Johnson Residence, Afternoon 12:55 pm 153

Milford Sheriff's Department, Afternoon 1:25 pm 162
Somewhere in the Pike County Wilderness 165

Chapter 14: A Friend in Trouble 175

Milford Sheriff's Department: Evening 9:30 pm 175
Jim Gold's House, Evening 9:42 pm 176
Milford Sheriff's Department, Evening 9:50 pm 179
Somewhere in the Pike County Wilderness 183
Milford Clinic, the next morning 8:00 am 184

Chapter 15: Painful Admissions and Cunning Plans .. 193

Todd Hunter's General Store, Morning 11:05 am 193
Somewhere in the Pike County Wilderness 201
Milford Sheriff's Department, Afternoon 1:00 pm 209
Jim's House, Afternoon 2:05 pm 216

Chapter 16: Even the Best Laid Plans 223

Somewhere in the Pike County Wilderness 223
Shaw's Bar, Evening 10:30 pm 232
Jim's House: The next morning at 10:03 am 238

Chapter 17: In Plain Sight 239

Milford Clinic, Morning 10:15 am 239
Milford Radio Station: Morning 10:45 am 248
Jim's House, Morning 11:05 255
Milford Sheriff's Department, Afternoon 5:05 255

Chapter 18: A Daring Rescue 259

Milford Sheriff's Department, Afternoon 5:35 259
The Marston Homestead, Evening 7:09 pm 263

Chapter 19: A Shocking Revelation 283
　Three Months Later 283

County Con: Road Runners

Jim Gold is a former FBI agent turned Private Investigator, currently living in a small town in Pennsylvania. Jim has earned the respect of the townspeople and the Sheriff's Department, but the peace and quiet is about to be disrupted by something sinister. A number of people travelling the back roads have been disappearing for a month, and the main suspect is a county police officer who pulls over the victims and kidnaps them. Jim is forced to involve himself in the case when a local girl he acts as the guardian angel for, Tracy Kean, is kidnapped. When his nemesis from the FBI shows up and takes over the case, Jim must work fast to save Tracy. But after a while, he starts to think that there's more going on, and the perpetrators are even more dangerous than anyone he's ever faced.

Written and owned wholly by Matthew James Colfer.

Chapter 1
DUI (Drinking Under the Influence)

In the wilderness of Pike County, Pennsylvania, the back roads leading through the trees have always been considered dangerous routes. Day or night, it often contained drunk drivers, hunters coming back from a good day, or local folks who don't have that much in the way of social skills.

A car was driving down the road; its occupants were four teenagers around the ages of eighteen and nineteen; their names were Derek, Jimmy, Tammy and Cassie. They were actually on their way to a night on the town in one of the big cities, but that hadn't stopped them from going into the nearest bar for a "quick" drink. Derek was the designated driver, so he had to stay sober, not that the desperation for a drink wasn't killing him as they traversed the night road, so dark that without proper lighting, you couldn't take your eyes off for a second.

"So then I said, bitch, I don't care who your dad is. I ain't holding your hand to cross the road, and that's that!" said Jimmy, already three sheets to the wind; Tammy and Cassie were the same.

"You actually said that to a five-year-old? All she wanted was someone to help her cross the road to the bus stop," said Tammy.

"I don't give a shit, I'm not a goddamn crossing guard. She can ask some other stranger to help her out; it's not my problem!" said Jimmy.

"Jimmy, your good-natured attitude makes the world proud," said Cassie.

"Hey, come on, D man, step on it; we gotta get to the club before all the hot chicks stop dancing."

"I'm going as fast as I can," said Derek without looking at Jimmy.

"Oh, come on, man, you can't still be mad about the whole drink thing," said Jimmy.

"How can I be mad when I'm not even wasted? That's when you see me mad," said Derek.

"Look, D, it's the whole designated driver thing; one of us needs to be sober enough to get us there. Once we arrive, you can drink to your heart's content and pass out in a motel like the rock stars do," said Jimmy.

"Look, I haven't had a drink in months, not since my dad caught me with his emergency whisky bottle. He put a padlock on the cupboard and said that if I touched one sip, he'd take his belt off," said Derek.

"Then what are you complaining about? Wouldn't your dad have known if you took a drink from the bar?" said Tammy.

"Of course, he'd know then. But I thought that since we're friends, you guys might have shared a little from those bottles you swiped from the bar when they weren't looking," said Derek.

"I mean, a little liquid courage and a show of love might actually help us get there faster, you know," said Derek.

"Okay, Derek, listen, I love you, so I'm going to help you out; come here," said Cassie as she took a big slurp from the bottle, held it in her mouth, and then moved over to Derek from the back and supposedly kissed him while also giving him the alcohol. Derek swallowed it as Cassie sat back down.

"WHOOOOO!!" shouted Derek as he put his foot down on the gas. This would have frightened most people, but everyone shouted the same, "WHOOOOO!!"

The car was now going even faster down the road; all the liquid courage meant that no one minded. But then, a sound suddenly filled the air, one that always sends teenagers into panic mode and eliminates all happiness. It was a police car's siren coming up in the rear-view mirror behind them. Derek had no choice but to pull over; everyone looked at each other. The girls quickly grabbed the two whisky bottles they'd been drinking from and hid them under the car seats, then they all took some deep breaths and wiped their faces, trying to hide their drunkenness.

The police car stopped behind them; it was the County Police. One officer, a young man in his late thirties, got out of the car and approached the teens. He came up to the driver-side window and knocked gently on it. Derek pressed the button to lower the window; the officer shined a flashlight at everyone as he leaned over a bit to see them.

"Good evening, how's everyone doing tonight?" said the officer.

"Um, uh, good, good officer, we're good," said Derek, trying to keep calm.

"Well, good. So, are you the driver of this vehicle, sir?" said the officer.

"Yes, yes, officer I....I am," said Derek.

"Well then, can I see your licence and registration?" asked the officer.

"Sure, sure thing, officer, one moment," said Derek as he had Jimmy open the glove compartment to get the vehicle registration, then reached into his wallet to get his licence.

Thankfully, it was legit, as was the registration. The car originally belonged to Derek's dad, but he gave it to him as a present for his 19th birthday last year. The officer scanned the paperwork intently with his flashlight; everyone tried to remain calm. Finally, the officer gave the paperwork back to Derek, who gave it to Jimmy to put in the glove compartment.

"Well, everything seems in order, so down to business. Do you know how fast you were going, sir?" said the officer.

"I....I admit I might have gone over the speed limit a bit back there," said Derek.

"A bit? I call doing 60 in a 30-mile-an-hour area more than a bit," said the officer.

"It was a mistake, officer, a terrible mistake. I greatly apologise; I'm not usually a lawbreaker," said Derek.

"You girls are dressed real pretty. Where are you all off to at this time of night?" said the officer.

Everyone started stuttering a bit before Tammy finally answered.

"It's Cassie's birthday!" said Tammy.

"Yeah, it's my birthday!" said Cassie, playing along.

"Oh sweet, how old?" asked the officer.

"Nineteen, officer," said Cassie.

"Nineteen, not a bad age. So you guys are on a road trip to celebrate?" said the officer.

"Oh no, officer. We're actually heading to a big club in the city. Yeah, we're going to dance crazy to loud music, meet girls or boys, you know, the works," said Jimmy.

"Any drinking?" asked the officer.

"Well....yes, but only once we're there, and I'm the designated driver, so I'm strictly teetotal," said Derek.

The officer was quiet for a moment; everyone just stayed still. Finally, he smiled.

"Well, alright then, as it's a special night for a beautiful girl, I'm going to let this slide. But don't let me catch you doing it again," said the officer.

"Absolutely, officer, thank you so much," said Derek.

"Then, in that case, drive safely. Oh, and happy birthday Cassie," said the officer.

"Thank you, officer!" said Cassie while fluttering her eyelashes.

The officer started walking away; everyone breathed a sigh of relief.

"Oh wait, sorry, just one more question," said the officer as he came back into the same position.

"No problem, officer, what's the question?" said Derek.

"Do you think I'm an idiot?" asked the officer.

Everyone looked at each other, confused.

"Um, is this a rhetorical question?" asked Derek.

"No, I'm serious. Do you guys think I'm an idiot?" said the officer.

"Ah, ha, ha, I'm sorry, officer, what are we talking about here?" asked Derek.

"I'm talking about the fact I can so obviously smell the alcohol on your breath. I'm talking about the whiskey bottles those girls are hiding under their feet, and I'm talking about the fact that just a few metres before I clocked you guys, you idiots clipped a deer!" said the officer.

"No, we didn't," said Jimmy.

"Yes, you did. Check the blood stains on the right side of the car!" said the officer as everyone looked, their faces filled with shock at the reality of what was happening.

"Oh shit," said Jimmy.

"I'd like you all to please step out of the car," said the officer.

"Now wait a minute, officer, there has to be a way we can work.....work this....." Derek couldn't finish as he didn't look well.

"You okay?" asked the officer.

"Yeah....yeah, I'm go-" Derek threw up; he got it out the window and right onto the officer's shoes.

No one made a sound as the officer stared at Derek. The sound of a car door opening came from the police cruiser as another officer got out; he was older and taller than the first one. But the younger officer raised his hand, telling him to stay where he was.

"Would you like us to get out of the car, officer?" asked Derek.

"Yes, please," said the young officer.

The teens all slowly got out of the car and stood together on the car's right side; they were approached by both the young officer and the older one. He didn't say a word, just stared at them.

He then turned on his own flashlight and approached each of the teens, shining the light in their eyes.

"They're drunk," said the older officer.

"Now, this really isn't looking good for you guys. It was bad enough when you were speeding, but driving under the influence, injuring wildlife and lying to a police officer (he tuts)," said the young officer.

"Please, officers, it's a terrible misunderstanding; we're not bad kids," said Jimmy.

"He's right; we just wanted a night out; we didn't mean any harm!" said Tammy.

"I'm sorry I lied about my birthday; just let us go, please!" said Cassie.

Both the officers looked at each other.

"I'm sorry too, kids, but a crime has been committed, and I can't let you drive these roads any further, not in the state you're all in. Marlon, let's cuff them," said the young officer as he and the older officer, who was now named Marlon, both got out several cuff sets.

The teens protested as they were cuffed and led to the police car, except for Derek.

"Put them in the back, Marlon; I just want to finish talking to this guy," said the young officer.

"Sure thing, Frank," said Marlon as he opened the door and pushed Jimmy, Tammy and Cassie into the back car seat.

Derek just stood there with his hands cuffed, and the young officer, now called Frank, was staring at him.

"You know what makes me sick about you teens? You're disregarding the road safety laws. What if that deer had been a person? What if it was a mother, or father or someone's child? Would you have simply brushed it off and pretended it never happened?!" said Frank, getting angry.

"I'm sorry, really I am; I'll take full responsibility, just.....just let us go," said Derek.

"I appreciate what you're trying to do, kid. So I'll tell you what, I'm in a good mood, so I'll accept that you've taken responsibility for tonight's crimes," said Frank as he took a few steps back from Derek.

"So you'll let us go?" asked Derek.

"Not exactly; you've taken responsibility. That means all the bad stuff is on your conscience, and I have a duty to perform," said Frank as he suddenly drew his gun.

Shock filled Derek's face, as did his friends.

"What are you doing?!" asked Derek.

"I'm doing my duty, keeping these roads safe from drunken filth like you. So if I were you, and you still want your freedom, you'd start running and get as far away from me as you can," said Frank.

Derek looked back towards his friends.

"I'll count to three," said Frank.

"One. Two!" said Frank as Derek started running down the road while still cuffed. The others started shouting for him to keep running as Frank took aim.

"Isn't he doing as you said?" asked Marlon.

"Yes, he is, but there's one problem....I can still see him," said Frank as he pulled the trigger; the gun went off, and Derek fell to the ground.

His friends screamed as Marlon thumped his fist against the window and shouted, "SHUT UP!!" they did as he said.

Frank walked to where Derek was, still crawling while bleeding from his wound; he took aim at the wounded kid.

"Please.....I'm....sorry....I'm sorry," said Derek, barely able to breath.

"Do me a favour, tell that to the deer when you see him," said Frank as he pulled the trigger and finished Derek.

Everyone wanted to scream again, but they stifled their cries and just burst into tears.

Frank retrieved the handcuffs, then picked up Derek's body and threw him into the trees. He then went back to the teen's car, opened the door, pulled the handbrake off and guided the car towards the trees. It left the road and slid down an embankment; there was a crashing sound as it hit something at the bottom.

Frank went back to Marlon and got into the police car with him. With the rest of the teens still cuffed in the back, he smiled.

"Relax, kids, we're going to a party" said Frank as the police car pulled away into the darkness.

Chapter 2
Another Day in Milford

The Next Day: Milford, Afternoon, 12:00 PM

The small town of Milford, also in Pike county, was a quaint place that was always bustling with activity. Not as much as in the cities, but you'd see people walking around, families, locals, hunters, stores selling their wares, food being served in the diner and the bar, cars and pickup trucks going back and forth, and the town law enforcement patrolling the streets and keeping the peace. It was a really nice place to live.

Near the edge of town was a small building that served as a radio station. Inside were at least two interview rooms with microphones, headphones and one recording studio where all the magic happened. This was where the Violet Show was hosted; Milford's radio show with interviews, music, call-ins, weather and other news updates were broadcast, run by an African American girl in her late twenties named Violet; the show name was her idea. Also helping her was a blonde bespectacled 20yr old caucasian girl named Eileen; she was the studio tech and Violet's roommate, doing an online college course and working part-time at the studio as a work placement, keeping all the equipment maintained and working during each show.

A music track was just finishing as Violet was ready for an interview with someone who was well-known in Milford and someone she had always been pleased to see. As Eileen gave the signal, Violet spoke into her microphone.

"Hello, people of Milford, this is Violet Hanson and welcome to the afternoon addition of the Violet Show!" said Violet as Eileen hit the button, which sounded the recorded audience noise.

"Today, we have a very special guest joining us. This will be a call-in interview, so if you have any questions to ask our guests, the phones will be open in just a second. This man came to our fair town nearly five years ago, and he's become someone we can trust and rely on. He's our town's first ever Private Investigator, you know him, we love him, it's Jim Gold!" said Violet as the recorded audience sounded again.

Jim sat just opposite Violet with his own microphone.

"Oh, oh please, you're too kind," said Jim, playing along to the audience cheering.

Jim was a white man in his late forties, his hair combed back from his forehead and curling at the ends.

"So Jim, how are you today?" asked Violet.

"I'm doing good, Violet; how are you?" replied Jim.

"I'm great, thanks. Now, Jim, today is actually a very special day, is it not?" said Violet.

"I think the harvest festival was last week, right?" said Jim as Violet laughed.

"No, silly, it's the five-year anniversary of when you first arrived in our fair town. Solving cases big and small in all that time, how does it feel?" said Violet.

"I don't think too much of anniversaries, actually. But I will admit that these last few years have shown me that I can still use my skill set to help people, and everyone in Milford has been so kind to me. I'm glad to have found somewhere that I fit in, especially after my previous job," said Jim.

"Oh yeah, didn't you used to work for the FBI in Washington DC?" asked Violet.

"That's right; it's not something I like to talk about, though. Nothing personal, just….you know," said Jim.

"That's okay, Jim, the past is the past, right?" said Violet as Jim nodded.

"Okay folks, the phone lines are now open, so if anyone has a question to ask our favourite PI, here's someone right now (she signals Eileen to put the caller through). Hello caller, you're live on the Violet Show," said Violet.

"Hello, Violet, it's Mrs Salazar," said a woman with a Spanish accent over the phone.

"Oh, hello, Mrs Salazar. Do you have a question for Jim?" said Violet.

"I do, yes. Mr Gold, I'm sorry to ask this because I know you just said you don't like to talk about it, but my son Gomez wants to join the FBI when he's older, and I don't know if I want him to. Can I just ask what it's like? It's okay if you don't want to," said Mrs Salazar.

"That's okay, Mrs Salazar; I'm happy to talk about how the FBI works; I just don't like talking about why I left, that's all. Well, the FBI obviously does good work, you know, we fight the drugs trade, serial killers, terrorists, and we do what we can to help save lives. But the downside is that you don't just need the skills; you also need the patience. You have to be able to head up an investigation and do thorough searching and evidence gathering; you can't just go around tackling people and waving a gun around at them. That just leads to courtrooms, inquiries and hard questions about your early life from Internal Affairs. Now, I'm not saying don't join; if that's his decision, then you have to support him. But the FBI has a much higher standing in society; they expect the best, so he needs to be ready to give it," said Jim.

"Thank you, Mr Gold; I'll think about what you said", Gomez suddenly said over the phone.

"That's okay, Gomez. Maybe instead of watching the TV shows, focus on the more serious ones or read a book or two on how the FBI operate; it'll help in the long run," said Jim.

"I will, thank you, Mr Gold," said Gomez.

"Yes, thank you, Mr Gold, good day", said Mrs Salazar as she put the phone down.

"Well, that was a very informative first call. I wonder if the others will be the same, oh, another caller. Hello caller, you're live on the Violet Show," said Violet.

"Hi, I don't really have a question. I just want to say that you're a very handsome man, Mr Gold, and I love you. I hope one day you'll marry me. Thanks. I love you!" said the caller as she put the phone down.

"Um, thank you, whoever that was. I'll make you a deal about the wedding; if you pick the cake and I pick the dress, we'll marry on Lovers Peak," said Jim.

"Well, it's not every day we get a marriage proposal through the radio. Except for the Morgans, of course, that was a wedding proposal to be recorded. Oh, another caller. Hello, you're live on the Violet Show," said Violet.

"Hey Violet, it's Todd Hunter," said Todd.

"Oh hey Todd, how's business at the General Store?" said Violet.

"Um, actually, things aren't too good at the moment; that's one of the reasons I called in. Jim, I could do with your help," said Todd.

"What's wrong, Todd?" asked Jim.

"I've had a break-in at my house; some ass-absolutely stupid person has broken into my shed. I know it doesn't sound like much, but there was something very valuable to me in there, and now it's gone," said Todd.

"Well, I'll tell you what, Todd. As soon as the interview is over and I've just collected something from my house, I'll come round and have a look," said Jim.

"I appreciate that, buddy; thanks a lot. Oh, love the show, Violet, you're a goddess, don't tell your uncle I said that, bye," said Todd as he put the phone down.

"Well then, informative answers, wedding proposals and case offers, this has been one very lucrative show. Now we're almost out of time, but I recall my uncle saying he wanted to chime in at the end of the interview, oh, that's him now. Hey Uncle Reg, oh sorry, I mean Sheriff," said Violet.

"Hey honey, I've just been listening to the interview. Glad they didn't bombard you with too many questions, Jim," said Sheriff Hanson.

"Yeah, me too, Sheriff," said Jim.

"So Sheriff, you said to me you had an important announcement for everyone," said Violet.

"Yes, I do. Now then, everyone, as some of you, but not all of you may know, a car carrying four local teenagers, Derek Johnson, Jimmy Pascal, Tammy Collins and Cassie Meadows, disappeared last night. They were last seen at Shaw's Bar before being asked to leave by Shaw himself for trying to purchase alcohol, despite being underage," said Sheriff Hanson.

"Witnesses and traffic cameras show their car leaving town by the back roads; since then, they haven't returned. The County Police have been informed and pledged to investigate as soon as possible. But this is now the fifth car to vanish along the back roads at night. The only advice I can give is to avoid travelling the roads when it's dark, and plan and time your journeys carefully. If you think it'll take too long to come either way, stay in town or find a motel or hotel for the night. Just be safe out there, everyone. Thanks, Violet; I'll pick you and Eileen up for dinner later this evening; love you, honey," said Sheriff Hanson.

"Love you too, Sheriff. So, folks, that's all we have time for; a big thanks again to our special guest for being on the show," said Violet.

"My pleasure, Violet," said Jim.

"So now it's time for the afternoon playlist and some call-in sessions in between. Until then, have a good day and be safe, everyone," said Violet as she signalled Eileen to cut her and Jim's mic. Then, she switched on the playlist.

Violet and Jim removed their headphones and stood up.

"Well, thank you for having me on your show, Violet. It's been fun, but it seems I now have a case opportunity," said Jim as he grabbed his jacket from the chair.

"No problem, Jim, you're welcome anytime. Jim, can I ask you something?" said Violet.

"Sure," said Jim.

"Why aren't you looking into the disappearances? I think someone with your skills might be invaluable," said Violet.

"Believe me, Violet, I wish I could, but like your uncle, I too am bound to respect the laws of jurisdiction. I can do things that happen in Milford and around most of the area outside, but once they get to Pike County, it's out of my hands," said Jim.

"It's a shame; Uncle Reg only told me about Derek going missing late this morning. His dad, Mr Johnson, came into the station and demanded a full search; he wasn't happy with what Uncle Reg told him," said Violet

"You're friends with Derek, aren't you?" asked Jim.

"Yeah, we've hung out together a lot over the years; I've even met the others he was with. Jimmy was a bit too into gangster rap for my tastes, though, but Derek is a good person; he just wants to grow up too quickly," said Violet.

"I'm sorry, Violet, I wish I could help, I do. But for now, just keep praying for him; he'll turn up," said Jim.

"Yeah, you're right," said Violet, feeling a little sad.

Jim went over and gave Violet a hug.

"I'll see you around, radio star," said Jim as Violet smiled. He then headed for the door.

"Oh Eileen, we'll marry on Lover's Peak, remember that?" said Jim as he left, revealing that the caller was actually Eileen.

"Eileen!" said Violet, laughing.

Eileen put her hands over her face as she laughed with embarrassment.

Jim left the radio station and started walking through the town to his home towards the centre, occasionally waving back to various people and making small passing-by conversations.

Jim wasn't your typical everyday PI. Like what was brought up in the interview, Jim was once an FBI agent working in Washington DC; he tackled drug lords, serial killers and biological terrorists; he received many commendations and was injured three times in the line of duty, thankfully nothing life-threatening. But something happened that he didn't like to talk about, something that was so bad he quit the FBI and moved away from DC entirely. He settled in Milford after finding it in a pamphlet about quiet country towns that were great places to retire. Jim took the opportunity and moved in the first chance he got. The funny thing is that Jim didn't intend to be a PI; he just wanted to settle into the quaint small-town life and live as he wanted. But only after his first week, a murder in the wilderness just outside of Milford shook the town for a bit.

A hunter by the name of Hicks Paxton was accused of murdering his best friend, Albert Long, during a hunting trip. It was revealed that Hicks' wife had been having an affair with Albert, and it'd all come out after Hicks found one of her earrings in the back of Albert's truck. When confronted, he confessed everything. Shortly after splitting off in different directions, Albert was shot through the neck; he died instantly. The bullet matched Hicks' rifle, and footprints indicated he was actually following Albert from a distance; Hicks was arrested and thrown in a cell pending trial.

Somehow, Jim's FBI past was discovered as Hicks' daughter, Jessica, came to Jim and begged him to help prove her father's innocence, while at first reluctant, he agreed. Jim made friends quickly with one of the deputies of the Milford Sheriff's Department, Joey Brandon. As the two of them investigated the murder, only a day later, Jim discovered that Jessica was right; Hicks had been set up by his own wife.

Apparently, Hicks' wife wanted nothing to do with him or Albert anymore; she was tired of the pair of them. She planted one of her earrings for Hicks to find, and after the argument, she killed Albert with a similar model rifle to the one Hicks used, then waited for the evidence to speak for itself. She'd be a free woman, but not anymore, thanks to Jim Gold. Hicks and Jessica showed their appreciation by offering Jim payment; he wasn't sure about taking it at first but finally gave in after realising that his own job prospects weren't yielding much.

Over the next few months, word spread about Jim, and people started coming to him whenever they had a problem. After his fifth case, Joey gave Jim the idea of getting a licence and becoming a Private Investigator for Milford, the first one they'd ever had. Surprisingly, Jim agreed and set up his office at home since he couldn't use any other space. Over the years, even during the months before he set up, the cases Jim got ranged from frivolous things like lost dogs and missing wallets to slightly more serious ones such as car thefts, break-ins and kids, both little and teenage, who missed their curfew.

Despite this not being the retired life he expected, Jim had grown to like it. He was away from the hustle and bustle of the big city; he was working a job that allowed him to help people and was well paid for it, and the people of Milford had come to appreciate and respect the things he did for them. Even Sheriff Hanson and the rest of the department took notice, and they came to accept him as part of the family, the small-town family.

Jim finally arrived at his house, a two-story with a sheltered porch and a garage. He did have a car, but he mainly used it for when he was travelling long distances; the rest of the time, he preferred to walk. Jim walked up the two steps to his front door, unlocked it with the key and went inside; he closed the door behind him. A number of letters had been put through the letterbox; he picked them up and looked at what they were. Nothing interesting offers on a big sale in the city, a couple of bills, but he was keeping up, and a few cards from friends in the FBI he kept in touch with.

His house was quite a nice one, a living room with a couch, an armchair and a 10-inch screen TV; it was actually a present from another client for finding out who was robbing his electronics store. The cabinet it was standing on held a collection of DVDs, either single or box sets, Private Eyes, Frankie Drake Mysteries, Agatha Christie's Poirot, Miss Scarlet and the Duke, Stumptown, the classics. His kitchen was a bit small, but it had the necessities like a refrigerator and a working stove/oven. He even had a table with a couple of chairs in there, so it also served as the dining room, not that he had many guests over, and most of the time, he'd eat out at the diner or Shaw's Bar.

He had a laundry room at the back and two bathrooms; the one upstairs was better equipped. He also had something of a backyard, which didn't get used much unless he was mowing the grass or needed a quiet place to think. Finally, he had the upstairs bedroom and another room that served as his "office", but he usually interviewed potential clients in the living room. The office was more his "Crime Lab", where he'd place his clues, review his notes, examine evidence and connect the dots. One particular board with a number of photographs and red string pinned all over was pushed to the far wall, but it was something Jim looked at often, something that was always on his mind and was, in fact, the whole reason why he left the FBI.

But Jim came back primarily to collect his notebook. He opened the drawer on the desk and lifted it out. Most people used notepads, but he felt he could fit more into a notebook. He also had a gun in there; it was registered to him, but he rarely took it out. Only if he was interviewing someone who was known to possess a firearm and has a short temper for the type of questions he was about to ask them. Jim felt reassured and proceeded to leave his house. There were a lot more mysteries as to the kind of life Jim had before coming to Milford, but that was for a later time.

Chapter 3
The Empty Safe

Todd Hunter's House: Afternoon 12:30 pm

Jim walked to Todd Hunter's house, which was on the East end of town. Todd was the owner of the town's General Store; he was a decent man but had a bit of a temper when pushed. Otherwise, he kept the store in good condition and didn't overcharge the locals or tourists. Jim walked up some stone steps to find Todd was waiting for him.

"Hey, there's my favourite PI!" said Todd as he gave Jim a pretty tight hug.

"Uh, good to see you too, Todd," said Jim as Todd released his grip.

"So, what's this break-in you told me about?" asked Jim.

"Come with me, I'll show you", said Todd as he started leading Jim around the back of his single-story bungalow.

"So when I came home last night, everything seemed normal. I had myself some wheat toast and marmalade, watched my TV show, Big Bang Theory, then went to bed and had a nice dream about having dinner with Cameron Diaz. She's such a good actor, you know, and very pretty too, I just don't know her type," Jim finally stopped Todd.

"Could we get back to the shed, please?" asked Jim.

"You're right, Jim; I'm sorry, my mother always said I talk too much for my own good," said Todd as they came to the shed.

"This morning, when I left to open the store, I didn't even think to check the shed. But when I wanted to get lunch at the diner, I realised I'd left my wallet at home. So I came back to get it, just took one glance at the shed, and found that," said Todd as he pointed at a broken padlock on the ground just outside the shed door.

Jim knelt down, pulled out a handkerchief, which he used to handle potential evidence carefully, and picked up the padlock.

"It's been cut alright; I'd say bolt cutters would be my guess", said Jim as he got back up.

"Did you check if anything was taken?" asked Jim.

"Yeah, I did; come inside," said Todd as he led Jim inside the shed.

There wasn't a lot to look at, just an assortment of gardening tools and equipment.

"What did they break in for, tools?" asked Jim.

"Not the tools", said Todd with some sadness as he went over to the lawnmower, pushed it to the side, and then pulled open a metal panel attached to the floor under it, revealing a hidden safe.

"How long have you had this safe?" asked Jim.

"Nearly fifteen years," said Todd as he opened the safe by twisting the combination lock. It was empty.

Jim knelt down to have a look inside.

"What was being kept in here?" asked Jim.

"Oh, about….$237,000," said Todd. Jim was surprised as he looked at Todd.

"$237,000?" he said.

"It's my nest egg; I've been doing it for fifteen years, hence why I got the safe installed. Every time I have a few spare dollars on the side, I put them in the safe. It contributes towards my retirement fund," said Todd as Jim got back up.

"Who else knows about this?" asked Jim.

"No one, just me and now you," said Todd.

"Did you see or hear anything last night?" asked Jim.

"Not really, no. It'd been a tiring day at the store, so once I had my wheat toast and watched Big Bang, I went to bed and was out like a light. Which led to my thrilling dream with Cameron Diaz, ha, ha……um, but no, I didn't see or hear anything," said Todd.

"Do you know anyone who'd do this to you?" asked Jim.

"Oh, I know who did this, Old man Wilson, the old codger. You know, it's been bad enough having to live with him just a mile out of town and argue for god knows how long over a land feud. But he's been planning this for years, to pull off a cunning and stealthy heist to relieve me of all my hard-earned money; I bet he's swimming in it right now!" said Todd.

"Todd, the guy is 87 years old," said Jim.

"So?" said Todd.

"He's got a limp," said Jim.

"So?" said Todd.

"And he has a heart condition. You really think that someone of that age with a bad leg and a fragile heart was able to pull off a money heist without doing something to give himself away or without the excitement being too much for his heart?!" said Jim as Todd thought for a moment.

"He might have" said Todd. Jim groaned.

"Look, you know what the crazy old man is like. Think about all the things he's done to me over the years!" said Todd.

"I thought you guys were finished with childishly pranking each other," said Jim.

"Yes, the Sheriff told us we weren't allowed to do it anymore, especially after the….chicken blood malfunction", said Todd.

"I was there, Todd; it wasn't funny," said Jim.

"Well, it was a little funny," said Todd.

"Okay, if you are the only person who knows about this safe, how could Old Man Wilson have found out about it?" asked Jim.

"Well, you remember all those times the Sheriff booked him for trespassing on my property?" asked Todd.

"The same amount that he booked you for trespassing on Wilson's property?" said Jim.

"That was different; I was just looking around, doing a little spying. That's nothing compared to all the tripwires he left in my yard or the compost he'd smear on the door handles," said Todd.

"He could have been mooching about, came into my shed and found the safe. Then thought, "I'll just help myself to Todd's hard-earned money", you see?" said Todd.

"Okay, aside from stating the obvious that the door was padlocked, even if Wilson had gotten into the shed and found your safe, how could he have gotten past the combination?" said Jim.

".....He might have been a safecracker in a former life," said Todd. Jim groaned again.

"Look, Jim, I know how this sounds, but I really need your help. You're the only one who can recover my retirement fund; you're my only hope," said Todd.

"Alright, I'll take the case," said Jim.

"Yes, you're the man, Jim!" said Todd as he fist-bumped him. They both left the shed.

"I will need to tell the Sheriff about this so he can send the deputies in for some evidence gathering," said Jim.

"Oh yeah, sure, I'll call him now if you like," said Todd.

"Are you going to tell them that crazy Old man Wilson is a former safecracker and that he broke into your shed without you knowing, so they need to go and arrest him right now?" asked Jim.

"Maybe you should call him," said Todd.

As Jim and Todd stopped by the steps, a rusty blue-shaded pickup truck was slowly driving past. Jim quickly realised it was Old Man Wilson, who was also doing a strange hand sign in an aggressive manner.

"I've told you before, that's not a threat, you crazy old codger!!" shouted Todd as the pickup left.

Jim just walked away quickly, not wanting to get into the middle of it.

Old Man Wilson's Property: Afternoon 1:00 pm

After writing everything down in his notebook, Jim walked the mile that led to Old Man Wilson's property. Most people called it a farm, but it was more like a large allotment with vegetable patches and greenhouses. Despite being outside of town, Wilson has always been considered a citizen of Milford, especially as his daughter lives in the town, too. Jim walked just to the edge of the property and spotted Wilson doing some gardening.

"Mr Wilson," said Jim as Wilson looked up.

"Glad to see someone still respects a man's property enough not to walk on it without an invitation," said Wilson.

"Come on up, Jim, I've just made myself some lemonade if you'd like a glass," said Wilson.

"I'd love one," said Jim as he started following Wilson up to the porch of his house.

Old man Wilson wasn't really a bad man, but he was known for having a short temper and being a bit grouchy, especially when it concerned his land. Wilson's daughter, Eileen, from the radio station, used to live with him, but at one point, his temper was so bad he hit her by accident. This led to a long time of no contact with her, and the stress was what led to his heart condition. After suffering an attack, Eileen arranged with the Sheriff to have custody visits with her father to slowly reconnect. It's worked pretty well so far; only more time will tell if their relationship is ever fully fixed.

Wilson sat down in a chair on the porch, and Jim sat in the one opposite. He poured some lemonade from a jug into two glasses and then handed one to Jim.

"Cheers," said Wilson.

"Cheers," said Jim as they clinked glasses and took a sip.

"That's pretty good, kind of sweet," said Jim.

"It's my daughter's recipe. She always makes some for me and brings it around, says it'll help "sweeten my nature.", ha, cheeky girl", said Wilson with a laugh.

"How are things with Eileen?" asked Jim.

"Good, so far, it's gone well. She's been to visit me, and I've been round to hers; we've had dinner and the occasional walk. We've tried to put the past behind us," said Wilson.

"So Jim, is this a social call, or are you buttering me up for business?" asked Wilson.

"I hate to say it, but business brought me here, and I'm afraid it's to do with your neighbour", said Jim.

"You know, when I saw you standing with Todd outside his house, I had a feeling that you'd soon be round. So come on, what's the stubborn jackass accusing me of this time?" said Wilson as Jim got out his notebook.

"Todd has hired me to investigate a robbery at his place. Before I get into details, I just have one question: did you know about Todd's hidden safe?" said Jim.

"He has a hidden safe?" asked Wilson.

"And I'll take your reaction that you didn't. Todd had a hidden safe installed nearly fifteen years ago to store his retirement fund. Someone broke into it," said Jim.

"Ah, and he thinks that I somehow pulled off a cunning and stealthy heist to relieve him of all his hard-earned money," said Wilson.

"Those exact words," said Jim as he and Wilson laughed a bit.

"You know, Jim, if anyone else had come onto my property and accused me of robbery, I'd send them away with their tail between their legs. But you're the kind of man I respect, and you've always been good to me and Eileen. Hell, I still remember you finding my pickup all those years ago. The Sheriff had mostly written her off, but you kept searching and brought the old girl back to me," said Wilson.

"Didn't you just forget to put the brake on, and she rolled away?" asked Jim.

"Yep, sounds like me," said Wilson with a laugh.

"So anyway, I'll tell you this: I hate Todd Hunter, hate him with every fibre of my being. Just because his house encroaches over the border of what's considered my land, it gives him a partial right to it. So if I ever want to sell or renovate the land,

I have to ask his permission, and he gets half the price if I do sell it," said Wilson.

"I admit the pranks were a bit much, but he trespassed on my land just as much as I did to him; he's stubborn, full of himself and basically a jackass. But, I would never do something as criminal and degrading as to break into a safe and steal money from him 'cause that'd hurt Eileen more than it'd hurt me," said Wilson.

"I believe you, Wilson; like you said, you wouldn't do anything to jeopardise your relationship with your daughter. But if you happen to know anyone else who had reason to hate Todd and even go as far as stealing from him, it'd really help me," said Jim as Wilson laughed.

"Todd likes to think he's loved by everyone. Just because his General Store, like the diner and Shaw's Bar, is one of the places that keeps the town prosperous and in the money. But I can think of one or two people who don't like the kind of man he is," said Wilson.

"I'd really appreciate their names, Mr Wilson," said Jim.

"Happy to help," said Wilson as he and Jim picked up their glasses and clinked them again.

Somewhere in the Pike County Wilderness

In a place that was cold and damp, Cassie began to regain consciousness. She quickly found that she was chained up to a wooden wall; looking around, she saw bales of hay and various farming tools; she seemed to be in some kind of barn. Cassie turned to find that Tammy and Jimmy were next to her and also chained to the wall; she used her leg to nudge Tammy and try to wake her up. After a moment, Tammy opened her eyes.

"Cassie, where….where are we?" asked Tammy.

"I…I don't know, some kind of barn. Last thing I remember, we were in the back of that cop car. Did they gas us?" said Cassie.

Tammy looked at Jimmy and did the same nudging Cassie did to wake him up.

"What….what's happening?" asked Jimmy.

"We've been abducted, Jimmy, remember the cops?" said Tammy.

"…..Oh god…..I thought I was dreaming…they really killed Derek, didn't they?" said Jimmy as tears filled his eyes. The same with Tammy and Cassie.

"Yeah, they did," said Cassie.

"Alright, we need to get out of here, 'cause I'm going to find and kill those guys!" said Jimmy as he started struggling with his chains.

"Jimmy, they're cops, and they were armed. They've most likely dealt with rage-infused teens like you before; you wouldn't survive!" said Tammy.

"I don't care; either I kill them with my bare hands, or I die trying. Either way, I'm satisfied," said Jimmy.

"Now come on girls, let's see if we can get free of these chains," said Jimmy as he kept struggling; Tammy and Cassie considered joining in.

But just then, the doors at the front of the barn opened. Two people entered; one was an older man with white hair and a shotgun, and the other was a kid in his late twenties with curly hair; he also had a shotgun. They came up to the teens and stood in front of them.

"Good to see y'all are awake, don't want you to miss all the fun we have planned," said the older man with a slight redneck accent; his name was Harlan.

"Please, sir, we're not bad people; we're just teenagers doing stupid and idiotic things. We're not a threat to you; if you let us go, we won't tell anyone anything, I swear!" pleaded Cassie.

"Sorry, little miss, but no, I cannot do it. Our mutual friends said we were to hold you all and have as much fun as possible, and that's what my boy and I intend to do," said Harlan.

"What are you going to do to us?" asked Tammy.

"Why have fun, of course. It's a party after all, didn't they tell you that?" said Harlan.

"I don't know if you realise, but those cops you're all buddy, buddy with shot my best friend right in front of us!" said Jimmy.

"Ah yes, they told us about that. Shame he wasn't faster, wasn't it?" said Harlan.

"Look, sir, our parents aren't rich, but they have money; combined together, they can reach a high price. If you ransom us, they'll pay whatever you want, then you can let us go!" said Cassie.

"Oh, little miss, I see what you're trying to do. But my boy and I aren't in this for the money; we just want to have fun," said Harlan as he motioned to his son to approach the teens while he aimed his shotgun at them.

"Now, my boy is going to undo your chains, and y'all are going to stand up. If you try anything, I'll blow your stomachs open and watch you bleed out, understand?" said Harlan.

The teens didn't say anything; they just waited for the man's son to undo their chains and stand them up.

"Now then, here's how it's going to work. Each of you gets three chances; the longer you keep your chances, the longer you stay alive. But if you waste your chances by pointlessly trying to attack us or escape, then your deaths won't be quick and painless," said Harlan.

"Unlike your friend, he got the easy, cowardly way out. He could have stood his ground and tried to help you, but instead, he ran, abandoned his friends and paid the price for it. Some friend, huh, too chicken shit to be a man!" said Harlan as Jimmy suddenly tried to charge him, but the son quickly grabbed him and pinned him to the wall with the shotgun in his face.

"You stupid, boy?!" said the son with a slightly stronger redneck accent; his name was Cletus.

"I can see that you're the hothead of the group, so as it's understandable, I won't deduct one of your chances for that.....failure you just did. But, you also get the honour of being first to have fun with me and my boy; let's take him inside," said Harlan as his son dragged Jimmy towards the entrance. Cassie and Tammy tried to follow, but Harlan stopped them.

"Stay calm, girls; your turn will come soon. Now, we'll let you wander around a bit, but remember three things. One, me and my boy know these woods like the backs of our hands; two, we're both armed and three, you're miles from any sort of civilization, so trying to escape will be fruitless. See y'all soon, girls," said Harlan with a creepy laugh as he left the barn and closed the doors; a locking sound was heard from outside.

"Cassie….." said Tammy while shaking.

"It's going to be okay, Tammy. Our parents will have realised we're missing and reported it to the Sheriff; they're probably looking for us right now," said Cassie.

"Cassie, we were in Pike County when we were snatched; that's out of the Sheriff's jurisdiction", said Tammy.

"Well, they will have told the County police, and they're probably searching for us now," said Cassie.

"Cassie, those cops were wearing the uniforms of the County police. Even if they are searching for us, those two will make sure they never look in this direction, wherever this is," said Tammy.

"They're going to kill us, aren't they?" said Tammy.

Cassie wanted to say something but instead remained silent. Because deep down, she was worried that Tammy was right.

Chapter 4
Guardian Angel

Shaw's Bar, Evening: 7:00 pm

Jim sat in Shaw's bar, the only real bar/restaurant you'd find in Milford. It was evening, and Jim had spent most of the day going around town and interviewing all the people who had reason to hate Todd Hunter. But despite the conversations lasting for what felt like ages, they all said the same thing. They knew nothing about Todd's hidden safe, and they'd never be stupid enough to steal from him. All in all, it was back to square one.

Jim was happily enjoying his evening dinner, a plate of fillet mignon with some potatoes and a few vegetables. This was the one item on the menu that Jim actually liked and stuck with since he arrived. A man in his sixties with white hair approached Jim. This was Albert Shaw, owner and proprietor of Shaw's Bar, which includes the roles of cook and bartender.

"How's the fillet going, Jim?" asked Shaw.

"Delicious as always, Shaw," said Jim with a bit in his mouth.

"Glad to hear it," said Shaw as he noticed some customers at the bar and went over to tend to them.

As Jim went back to his meal, a younger man at the age of thirty with a neat haircut entered the bar, wearing the uniform of the Milford Sheriff's Department. This was Deputy Joey Brandon, Jim's first and best friend since he arrived in Milford five years ago. Joey saw where Jim was sitting and went over to him; he sat down in the opposite seat.

"Hey, Jim," said Joey.

"Joey, hey, how did it go at the crime scene?" asked Jim.

"Well, me and the deputies went over Todd Hunter's property with a toothcomb, we bagged the padlock and managed to get some prints off the safe's combination dial. A lot of them probably belonged to Todd, but there were a couple that didn't look right. Anyway, it's all been sent to the forensics lab, and they gave the whole "We'll get back to you as soon as we can" sentence " said Joey.

"I know how that feels; well, at least it's in the works. Did you find anything else?" said Jim.

"No, nothing really, no footprints, no DNA samples. Whoever pulled this off knew what they were doing and took great care not to leave even the slightest incriminating sample," said Joey.

"Did you have much luck with your interviews?" asked Joey.

"Not really, either. Old man Wilson is clear for one, with his leg, his heart and Eileen, he wouldn't do something that foolish," said Jim.

"Yeah, if it had been him, this would have been the shortest case you've ever had", said Joey.

"Almost as short as the case of the runaway kitten. The answer is hiding under little Lisa's bed to escape that last night's thunderstorm," said Jim.

"Ha, yeah. So, do we have any suspects?" asked Joey as Jim shook his head.

"Questioned five people, and they all said the same thing; they hate Todd for their own reasons, but they knew nothing about the safe or the $237,000 he was storing in it. And they all made it clear that they wouldn't go as far as stealing from him," said Jim.

"So it's back to square one then," said Joey.

"Afraid so," said Jim as he finished his meal.

"You know Jim, since I met you for the last five years, you have come into Shaw's bar and eaten the exact same meal every evening. Why is it that you never want a change?" said Joey.

"Nothing wrong with a routine, Joey. If you like something, you stick with it, helps you stay sane," said Jim.

"Yeah, but it's like in the diner too. Every time I've come to see you there, you've always had an omelette for breakfast, nothing else, just the omelette and a bit of toast sometimes," said Joey.

"Joey, there's no real reason for doing anything. A person likes a routine; that's all there is. It may seem repetitive, but you can't fault a person for liking to do the same thing all the time," said Jim.

"Might get a bit boring, though?" said Joey.

The door to the bar opened, and a blonde-haired girl in her early twenties entered. Joey saw and recognised who it was instantly.

"Isn't that Tracy?" asked Joey as Jim turned to look.

Tracy Kean was a resident of Milford, currently living with her mother. She was dolled up to look really pretty.

"Yeah, it is," said Jim, as a young boy in what looked like his late teens. He entered the bar, put his arm around Tracy, and walked her to the bar.

"And it looks like she has a date," said Joey.

Tracy's date had short black hair and was wearing a black leather coat.

"I don't like the look of him," said Jim.

"What, what do you mean?" asked Joey.

"There's something about him. Look at the way he's dressed. Is he supposed to be a biker, or is he trying to look like a bad boy?" said Jim.

"Maybe he's just trying to impress her," said Joey.

"Yeah, I remember the last time someone did that, and the result wasn't good", said Jim as he saw the boy put his hand on Tracy's leg.

"That's it," said Jim as he started to get up.

"Jim, don't," said Joey.

"I'm not going to hit him; I'm just going to talk with him," said Jim.

"Look, Jim, I know you feel some compulsion to be Tracy's protector. But she's her own woman, and you embarrassing her isn't going to help things," said Joey.

"I'm just going to talk to him, that's all. No embarrassment necessary," said Jim.

"You need backup?" asked Joey.

"I'll signal you if I do," said Jim as he walked towards the bar.

"Wait, what's the signal?" asked Joey as Jim had already left.

Tracy and her date seemed to be having a good laugh about something. But the laughter died down as Jim came over.

"Evening, Tracy," said Jim.

"Jim, hey, um, evening. Uh, Leon, this is Jim Gold, the guy I was telling you about," said Tracy.

"No way, the private investigator; it's an honour to meet you, sir," said Leon as he extended his hand; Jim reluctantly shook it.

"Pleasure's all mine," said Jim.

"Leon is from New York; he's down here on vacation. I've just been showing him around Milford," said Tracy.

"And I couldn't have asked for a better tour guide," said Leon as Tracy laughed a bit.

"A city boy? So tell me, Leon, what do you get up to in the big city?" asked Jim.

"To be honest, I'm kinda in between jobs right now; I mean, my parents are always on my case about what I'm doing with my life. But I'm thinking, it's my life, and I'm a free spirit; I can do whatever I want with myself," said Leon.

"Oh, so your parents are okay with you vacationing on your own then?" asked Jim.

"Yeah, of course they are. Like I said, free spirit," said Leon.

Tracy wasn't looking happy.

"Look, his parents are okay with him being here, so let's just leave it at that," said Tracy.

"Oh, okay, so your mother knows you're out with this guy, right?" asked Jim.

"It's not like I'm on curfew, Jim. I'm 23 years old, and I needed to get away from my mom for a while; okay, so can we just get along?" said Tracy.

"Sure," said Jim.

"So Leon, have you ever been in trouble with the law before?" asked Jim as Tracy facepalmed.

"Excuse me?" said Leon.

"Jim, can I talk to you for a second over there?" asked Tracy.

"Of course," said Jim as Tracy got up from her seat.

"I'll be back in a minute", Tracy said to Leon as she led Jim to the other end of the bar.

"Okay, Jim, what the hell, why are you grilling Leon?" asked Tracy.

"I'm not grilling him; I'm just trying to get to know him," said Jim.

"Have you been in trouble with the law recently?" That's what you ask someone when you suspect they've committed a crime," said Tracy.

"Has he committed any crimes?" asked Jim.

"That's not what I meant. Look, Jim, Leon has been really nice to me; okay, he hasn't done or said anything sexist or made me uncomfortable; he's actually really sweet," said Tracy.

"Then why the whole bad boy biker look?" asked Jim.

"People can dress like the baddest criminal and still actually be decent; they don't always need suits and ties," said Tracy.

"Look, I don't need a babysitter, okay, and I especially don't need my mom getting on my back and being a control freak," said Tracy.

"Hey, your mom's not a control freak, don't you call her that. She loves you very much," said Jim.

"You haven't seen her recently, Jim; she's getting worse. But that's something for another time. Jim, this is my life. I know how to live it, and no offence is intended, but I don't need your help. You're not my dad!" said Tracy as she walked away and went back to where Leon was sitting.

Jim was slightly bemused as he considered going back to his seat.

"Everything okay?" asked Leon.

"It's fine," said Tracy with a slight frustration in her voice.

The barmaid brought a tray with a lemonade for Tracy and a pint of beer for Leon.

"Thank you, my dear," said Leon as he went to take a sip, but Jim stopped him.

"Wait a minute, let's see your ID," said Jim.

"I beg your pardon?" said Leon.

"I'd very much like to see your ID so I can make sure you're old enough to be drinking that," said Jim.

"Oh please, god no," said Tracy quietly to herself.

"But I already showed it to the barmaid.....okay, you know what, fine, here it is, happy now?" said Leon as Jim took the ID and held it closer to his eyes.

"Mr Shaw, take a look at this; what do you think?" said Jim as he handed the ID to Shaw and he examined it.

"Why, I do believe this is a fake, Jim," said Shaw.

"Fake?!" said Tracy with surprise.

Shaw handed the ID back to Jim.

"Flaunting your fake ID isn't going to earn you any friends around here, Leon. Even a city boy like you wouldn't be that stupid," said Jim.

"Look, I don't know who you think you are. Is there a problem here?" Leon got up to try to intimidate Jim, but he was interrupted as Joey approached them.

"Uh, no, no problem here, officer," said Leon.

"Well, there's about to be, Leon, is it? Take your city boy ass out of here, you're barred!" said Shaw.

"Mr Shaw, please," said Tracy.

"Tracy, sweetheart, I'm sorry. You're still welcome here anytime, but your boyfriend has to go," said Shaw.

"Let's go, Leon, come on," said Tracy as she started pulling Leon towards the door, but he stopped partway.

"This isn't over, Mr Gold. I know people in the city, people who can make life miserable for you!" said Leon.

"Is that a threat I just heard?" asked Joey.

"Legal action, I was talking about lawyers, not thugs," said Leon.

"You really want to go to the trouble of hiring lawyers to help you recover your fake ID because you were hoping the locals would be idiot hillbillies?" asked Jim.

"That's not what I said!" said Leon.

"Leon, come on. Seriously, Jim!" said Tracy as she finally pulled Leon out the door, and they headed down to the right.

"Here you are, Mr Shaw, you better hang on to this," said Jim as he gave the fake ID to Shaw.

"Thanks, Jim, I'll add it to the collection," said Shaw.

"Well, that went well," said Joey.

"Yeah, at the very least, Tracy seemed surprised by the fake ID. That's one point towards her realising Leon's bad news," said Jim.

"Even if she hates you for it?" asked Joey. Jim didn't answer that.

But he did notice four thuggish-looking men walk in front of the glass windows, then point and run in the direction Leon and Tracy went in.

"You saw that, right?" asked Jim.

"Yeah, I didn't like the look of them, and wasn't that the direction Tracy and Leon went?" Jim finished Joey's sentence.

"Oh crap, I think there's about to be trouble," said Joey.

"You need backup?" asked Jim.

"Hell yeah, Mr Shaw, call the Sheriff!" said Joey as he and Jim ran out the front door.

The two of them ran towards a small alley that was next to the bar; they started hearing raised voices. One was Leon, but the other sounded like one of the thugs. They took cover by the entrance and peeked around the corner; two of the thugs had Leon pinned against one of the dumpsters and occasionally hit him after he spoke. Another thug had Tracy pinned to the wall just opposite them, and the final thug was acting like the ringleader, asking questions that sounded like, "You thought you could get away with it?" and "You owe us!" before hitting Leon again. Joey pulled out his gun and nodded to Jim. The two of them then charged into the alley.

"Milford Sheriff's Department, everybody, stop what you're doing!" shouted Joey as the ringleader suddenly pulled a gun and aimed it at him; Joey aimed back.

"Whoa, don't be an idiot, buddy!" said Joey.

"This has nothing to do with you. We just have some business to discuss with him!" said the thug.

"You're holding a citizen of Milford in an aggressive manner; let her go and surrender peacefully!" said Joey as he and the thug soon began overlapping their words.

Things were getting tense. Jim was trying to assess the situation and figure out what to do. He looked over to Tracy, who looked back at him with a frightened expression and silently whispered his name. Jim's guardian angel act kicked in.

He slowly approached a small bin with a metal lid. When he was close enough, he looked ahead and shouted, "Sheriff, now!"

The thugs looked behind them, but no one was there. Jim quickly grabbed the bin lid and threw it like a frisbee at the thug with the gun. It hit him on the head and knocked him down before he could react. Jim ran into the alley and tried to go for Tracy, but one of the thugs holding Leon broke away and got in his path; he swung for Jim, who dodged the throws, then punched him in the face and grabbed him; the thug did the same. The second thug punched Leon in the stomach before running to help his friend.

"Behind you!" Tracy shouted.

Jim ducked as the thug swung a punch and hit his friend instead. Jim kicked the thug in the stomach, and then, as the thug charged him again, Jim grabbed the guy and flipped him over. The thug he was just fighting tried to throw a punch, but Jim blocked it and hit him back. The thug that was flipped saw the gun on the ground and went for it.

"Don't even think about it!" said Joey as he stopped the thug.

Jim then grabbed the thug he was fighting, lifted him over his shoulders in a sort of fireman's lift and threw him into the open hatch on the dumpster. Jim turned around, but as the thug tried to get out, he hit the dumpster and caused the lid to fall on the guy.

The final standing thug holding Tracy let go of her and pulled out a knife as he went for Jim.

"You scared, old man?" said the thug, trying to act tough.

"You think that butterknife scares me? I once fought a Mexican cartel boss with a machete the size of your arm, and funnily enough, he used it to remove people's arms," said Jim.

"Then come at me, old man; what are you waiting for?" said the thug as he was suddenly hit over the head with another dustbin lid and fell to the ground unconscious.

Jim looked up as Tracy was holding the lid before she threw it to the ground. He went over to her.

"You okay?" asked Jim.

"Yeah, a little shaken, but yeah," said Tracy.

"Not bad," said Jim, looking at the unconscious thug.

"Thanks," said Tracy with a smile.

Leon started getting back up.

"Tracy, you alright, babe?" said Leon just as Jim grabbed him and threw him up against the second dumpster.

"Oh, not again!" said Leon.

"Why were those guys after you?!" asked Jim.

"I don't know what you mean!" said Leon.

"I heard what they said, "You thought you could get away with this" and "You owe us". Now you better start telling the truth, because if you don't, then you're next in the dumpster!" said Jim.

"Okay, okay, alright, look, the thing is....I kinda owe those guys money," said Leon.

"WHAT?!!!" shouted Tracy.

"I was jumped in an alley, pinned to the wall, and nearly had my face smashed in, all because you owe someone money?!" asked Tracy.

"It's a little more complicated than that," said Leon.

"I don't believe this. I could have looked past the fake ID, but you put me in danger. I thought you were different, Leon," said Tracy.

"Tracy, come on babe-I'm not your babe!" Tracy interrupted Leon.

"You're just like the other jerks. Jim, I'm really sorry.....can you please take me home?" said Tracy as Jim smiled.

"Sure thing, Tracy," said Jim as they both walked out of the alley. The sound of approaching sirens could be heard as they did.

"Tracy, wait-" Leon tried to go after them but was stopped when Joey grabbed his arm and threw him against the dumpster again.

"Oh, come on!" said Leon.

"You're not going anywhere, buddy; you're under arrest," said Joey.

"Arrest for what?" asked Leon.

"Using a fake ID is one thing, but putting a life at risk is another," said Joey.

Jim and Tracy exited the alley as three police cars pulled up, and the Sheriff got out of one of them. Sheriff Hanson was a man in his sixties with shoulder-length wavy grey hair.

"Sorry, we came as quickly as we could," said Sheriff Hanson.

"They're all yours," said Jim as he and Tracy walked past.

Sheriff Hanson went into the alley with his deputies and found the carnage left behind.

"Well, I'll be damned," said Sheriff Hanson with a chuckle.

"Hey, Sheriff, I could do with a hand here, oh and there's one more in the dumpster", said Joey.

"Of course there is. Alright, everyone, let's round them up," said Sheriff Hanson as he and deputies started picking up the beaten thugs and cuffing them. They didn't resist; they knew they'd been bested.

<u>Tracy Kean's House: Evening 7:15 pm</u>

Jim walked with Tracy down the street towards her house. It gave them some time to talk.

"God, I really thought Leon was different, not like the other jerks I've dated," said Tracy.

"So it was a date then?" asked Jim.

"Well, I may have been kinda hoping it'd develop into one. You know, back when I thought he was a sweet guy and a free spirit," said Tracy.

"Listen, Jim, I'm really sorry for what I said to you back at the bar. It was mean and nasty and totally uncalled for," said Tracy.

"Water under the bridge, Tracy, and it's not like your words weren't true; I'm not your dad," said Jim.

"Well, you could be an uncle," said Tracy.

"I can live with that," said Jim as he and Tracy laughed.

"Look, I'm sorry I'm always butting in at times, but I'm just trying to look out for you," said Jim.

"I know, and no matter how many times I may hate or resent your help, deep down, I appreciate it. But Jim, you have to let me grow up; I have to learn things my way," said Tracy.

"I'm forever grateful for when you saved my life five years ago, but that was another time I was younger and foolish. Now that I'm in my twenties, I need to learn and grow up myself. Sometimes you have to get knocked down a few times before you realise you're doing something wrong," said Tracy.

"Well, I'd prefer that it didn't happen, but I respect that analogy," said Jim.

"Tracy, back in the bar, you said something about your mother getting worse," said Jim.

"It's been a really hard few years for her, Jim. What with that business with the photographer and then dad leaving her, she's tried to pick up the pieces, and it's just too much for her," said Tracy.

"Sometimes she gets angry over the littlest thing. She over-stresses herself, and even though I try to do my bit to show she's loved and cared for, she doesn't even notice it half the time," said Tracy.

"Has she ever gotten physical?" asked Jim.

"Oh no, of course not," said Tracy as Jim stopped her walking.

"Tracy, has your mother ever gotten physical with you?" asked Jim.

"....There have been some close calls, but she's never actually done it. Plus, she wouldn't hurt me; she's my mom," said Tracy.

"Look, Tracy, why don't you come and stay the night with me? We can watch Private Eyes together," said Jim.

"I do actually like that show. But no, it's okay; if I don't go home, then Mom will freak out and call the Sheriff. I'll be fine," said Tracy.

Jim wanted to say more, but Tracy was a determined young woman. He finally gave in and walked her the rest of the way to her house.

The door opened, and a woman in her late fifties and looking a bit roughed up came out; this was Tracy's mother.

"Where have you been? I've been worried sick about you!" said Miss Kean.

"Mom, I told you earlier I was going out for a bit. I made sure you knew where I was," said Tracy.

"Well, yes, but you still could have called; I was about to ring the Sheriff. Jim, thanks for bringing her home, love; I do hope she wasn't any trouble," said Miss Kean.

"No, Miss Kean, she wasn't any trouble. Tracy had just gone for a walk around the town, and she bumped into me taking a stroll myself, so the two of us went together. We talked and laughed, had a quick lemonade in Shaw's, and then I walked her home," said Jim.

"I'm sorry, Mom, I lost track of time", said Tracy.

"Well, at least you weren't by yourself, I suppose. Have you eaten?" said Miss Kean.

"No, Mom," said Tracy.

"Well then, you can make yourself a sandwich; there's some stuff in the kitchen," said Miss Kean.

"Yes, Mom, and thank you, Jim, for the walk," said Tracy.

"You're welcome, kiddo, and hey (he reaches into his coat, pulls out a business card with his number on, and hands it to Tracy). Call me if you need anything," said Jim.

"I will," said Tracy as she hugged Jim, and he hugged back.

Tracy then went inside with her mom. Jim walked away and in the direction of his home; it'd been a long day.

Milford Sheriff's Department: Evening 9:00 pm

The Milford Sheriff's Department was quite a sizable building. Mostly, the inside was taken up with an assortment of desks for the deputies to field calls and file paperwork, a couple of holding areas for the criminal element, drunks and drug users and the rest was interview rooms, the archive and the armoury.

Joey came out from the holding area after putting the thugs in a cell for the night; they'd interview them in the morning. He thankfully had help from Min Lao, one of the only female Chinese deputies in Milford, but she was never rebuked or marginalised for who she was; the Milford family looked out for one another.

"Thanks for the help back there. I thought I'd have to pick that guy up by his belt and toss him inside," said Joey.

"No problem, though it would have been fun to see you do that," said Min with a chuckle.

"Well, I've been getting my exercise, so maybe next time", said Joey as he looked across the main area of the department and saw Leon walking towards him without cuffs on or an escort.

"The hell?" said Joey.

"See ya, Scrappy," said Leon as he walked past and slapped Joey's shoulder. With confused looks, Joey and Min approached Sheriff Hanson.

"Sheriff, what gives? Where's Leon going?" asked Joey.

"Leon Thornberg is free to go, Joey," said Sheriff Hanson.

"What, why, what about the charges?" asked Joey.

"The fake ID is a slap on the wrist. Now, we could have had him for endangering a life if we'd had time to get Tracy's statement," said Sheriff Hanson.

"So what happened?" asked Min.

"I made the mistake of letting him have his phone call. He put us through to one of those big city lawyers you hear about in the news. Apparently, he's "good friends" with his parents. Anyway, he threatened major legal action if we didn't release Leon, so, yeah," said Sheriff Hanson.

"Joey, it might be best if someone tells Jim about this so that he doesn't go all vigilante on us. Not that he does, but best not give him a reason to start," said Sheriff Hanson.

"Yeah, yeah, I'll go to his house and tell him," said Joey as he walked away.

"It's not your fault, Sheriff," said Min.

"Yeah, keep saying that enough times and maybe I'll start to believe it," said Sheriff Hanson as he walked away, too.

Min could feel the Sheriff's pain; this wasn't the first time he was forced to let someone go, and it wasn't the first time he had to live with it.

Chapter 5
Runaway

Jim Gold's House: Evening 9:10 pm

Jim sat on the sheltered porch of his house, drinking a couple of cold beers he kept on the side for when he needed one. Sometimes, it'd be when he'd just solved a case, done some good, or if he just needed to forget something, even if it wasn't permanent. Joey arrived on foot and approached the porch; Jim spotted him.

"Joey, come on over," said Jim.

"Hey Jim, got the beers out?" said Joey.

"Nothing like a good night's work to warrant a beer, right?" said Jim as he saw the expression on Joey's face.

"What's wrong?" asked Jim.

"The Sheriff had to let Leon go", said Joey, expecting Jim to go raving mad, but he didn't.

"You don't seem surprised," said Joey.

"Well, what did we expect, Joey? He's a spoiled rich kid who thinks that because his parents know so many lawyers, he's untouchable," said Jim.

"Yeah, that's what happened. Hey, how did things go with Tracy? " said Joey.

"Good. She apologised for what she said. I walked her home, and she seemed happy," said Jim.

"You really care about her, don't you?" said Joey.

"I do. I know she's right about me not being her dad but at times...I do think of her as the daughter I wish I could have had," said Jim.

"Well, I know she cares about you too," said Joey.

"Alright, come sit down and have a beer with me, Joey," said Jim as he picked out a bottle from the six-pack.

"I shouldn't, really, I'm still on duty...oh what the hell, just the one," said Joey as he took the beer and sat down. He opened it and took a sip.

"So, um, I've been meaning to ask. Does Tracy ever talk about.....Gary Phillips?" said Joey.

"She's mentioned him by profession, the photographer, but that's it," said Jim.

"I know it was five years ago. But I still can't believe that we let the slimy scumbag into our town and that we believed him when he said he was looking for models for a fashion magazine," said Joey.

"Instead, he roofied all the poor girls who went to him and, in their confused states, made them pose in skimpy underwear and revealing clothes for a porn site. And for a month, a whole month, we had no idea what he was doing!" said Joey.

"Then you came along, and you managed to take down that bastard," said Joey.

"I still spent two weeks investigating him, Joey," said Jim.

"Well yeah, but still, you did a good thing for Milford getting that scumbag arrested. And I know that if you hadn't found him when you did, Tracy might've been in an even worse state than she was then," said Joey.

"I'm just glad I got to her in time," said Jim.

"Hard to believe that Tracy was only eighteen when that happened," said Jim.

"Yeah, and then a year after, her dad left. That family's been through so much stress; she's actually lucky to have you as her guardian angel," said Joey.

"Yeah, but sometimes guardian angels have to know when to let them grow up on their own. It's the way of life, after all," said Jim.

"To growing up," said Joey.

"To growing up," said Jim as they clinked their bottles and entered a relaxed evening state.

Tracy Kean's House: Evening 10:05 pm

Tracy's house wasn't much to look at. A two-story building with a general living space inside. Despite her mother's condition, it was kept in good shape for the most part.

Tracy came out of the kitchen after doing all the dishes. She liked doing certain household chores to help her mother.

"Mom, I've just finished the dishes," said Tracy as she saw her mother in the living room, sitting down and not saying a word.

Tracy carefully went in.

"Mom, are you okay?" asked Tracy as she saw her mom was holding a pack of cigarettes.

"Are these yours?" asked Miss Kean

"Mom, I can explain," said Tracy.

"I found these in your jacket; are they yours?" said Miss Kean.

"Mom, I'm not smoking!" said Tracy.

"I didn't ask that; I asked if these cigarettes were yours," said Miss Kean.

"No, Mom, they're not; I was just….holding them for a friend," said Tracy.

"A friend, huh? Well, which friend? Was it Jimmy Pascal?" asked Miss Kean.

"Mom, you know Jimmy's missing," said Tracy.

"I know that I'm not stupid. He could have given you these to "hold onto" before he up and vanished. Now, are they his?" said Miss Kean.

"Yes, they are," said Tracy.

"LIAR!!" shouted Miss Kean.

"Mom!" said Tracy.

"Did you really think you could lie to me that I wouldn't think Jim was covering for you? I know you were with somebody tonight because I have friends in this town, too," said Miss Kean.

"Okay, yes, I'm sorry I lied, but I didn't want you to worry. Besides, I want nothing more to do with that guy, and Jim was there, so I was fine," said Tracy.

"You think that you can just lie to me and expect me to be okay with it? I'm disappointed, young lady; just wait until your father gets home," said Miss Kean as she walked out of the living room and into the hallway; Tracy followed.

"Mom, Dad's not here anymore; he left, remember?" said Tracy as her mom just stared at her.

"I'm going out for a smoke," said Miss Kean.

"Mom, you haven't smoked in years; you quit, remember?" said Tracy as she touched her mother's arm.

"Let go of me, and quit saying remember! I'm in control of my faculties, unlike you, it seems," said Miss Kean as she tried to walk away, but Tracy reached out for her again.

"Mom, please-AAGH!!!" Miss Kean turned and backhanded Tracy in the face.

Both of them were quiet as Tracy's face was bright red with a small cut. Tracy burst into tears and ran upstairs to her room.

"Tracy, I'm sorry, I'm sorry!!" shouted Miss Kean, but the door slammed shut.

Miss Kean had her own tears; she'd done something she'd never once considered doing, and now it was forever burned in her mind.

Tracy locked herself in her room; she fell onto her bed and started crying from both the pain on her face and what her mother had just done. Things had been bad since Tracy's dad left, cutting off all contact shortly after he did. Miss Kean eventually hired Jim to find him and convince him to keep paying child support, which he refused to do. This was the one time Jim ventured beyond Milford and managed to track down Tracy's father, then reason with him into paying for child support, and he agreed.

Tracy picked herself up and stared at a family picture on her desk; it was of her, Mom and Dad, a happier time. But this filled Tracy with anger as she flung the picture at the wall, and it smashed; she started crying again until something caught her eye. Another picture on her desk was of her and Jim. Tracy's dad used to take her fishing every few years; since he left, it felt like it wasn't going to happen, but Jim offered to take Tracy with him, and they had a surprisingly fun time together. Tracy smiled slightly, then noticed the business card with Jim's number and address on it. She quickly pulled herself together, grabbed a spare coat and a pair of shoes from under her bed, put them on, then opened her bedroom window and climbed down the drainpipe; she'd done it before, then she sneaked away from the house.

Downtown Milford: Evening 10:15 pm

A few minutes later, Tracy was walking through town in the direction of Jim's house. She was worried about how he would react to her bruise, especially after she'd basically sworn to him that her mother would never hit her. Tracy always knew that her mother wasn't well, but didn't want her to be sent off to a hospital or care home, given she was the only family she had left. A pair of headlights filled the road in front of Tracy as a yellow model sports car, like what you'd see in a drag race, slowed down and started driving next to her; the driver was Leon Thornberg.

"Tracy, you okay? Tracy, it's me, Leon," said Leon.

"Go away, I'm not talking to you," said Tracy.

"Look, Tracy, I'm sorry about the thugs, I really am. I didn't know they'd come all the way down here to find me," said Leon.

"Well, that's what happens when you make deals with loan sharks," said Tracy.

"No, Tracy, I don't owe them money; it's my parents that owe them; those guys just came down and threatened me to get to them. I only made it seem like it was me because I didn't want to drop them in it, plus that PI friend of yours looked like he was ready to catapult me out of town," said Leon.

Tracy finally stopped walking as Leon stopped his car; she turned to face him.

"Maybe I should have encouraged him. Because in the last few hours, you've tried to trick my friends with a fake ID, I've been pinned to a wall and threatened with violence, and to top it all off, I just got into a fight with my mother because she thought those cigarettes you asked me to hold onto were mine!" said Tracy.

"What happened to your face?" asked Leon. Tracy didn't answer.

"Look, I'm going to Jim's, okay? Don't follow me and don't talk to me, or else I'll tell him you're harassing me," said Tracy.

"Tracy, I don't expect you to believe me or forgive me. But let me try and make it up to you; let me take you for a drive," said Leon as Tracy scoffed.

"Please, it's not a kidnapping; it's an invitation. There's this really nice spot I'd like to show you, and it's a lovely night, too. I'll even take you back to Jim's afterwards or now if you don't want to come, please," said Leon.

Tracy thought for a moment; she knew that this was wrong, but so much pain had filled her that, at that moment, she didn't care. Tracy opened the door and climbed into the car; she quickly put on her seatbelt.

"One hour, that's your lot, then you take me to Jim's. If you try anything, I'll castrate you," said Tracy.

"Scouts Honour", said Leon as he put his foot down, and the car sped towards and then out of the town exit.

The Back Roads of Pike County, Evening 10:25 pm

The car was soon out on the back roads, the headlights still bright and doing a solid 40mph. Leon was smiling to himself while Tracy just sat quietly, occasionally rubbing her bruised face.

Finally, after a while of what felt like breaking the speed limit, Leon pulled down a small side road and came to a large lake in front of them. It glowed brightly because of the stars in the sky; Tracy couldn't help being amazed.

Leon switched off the car.

"What do you think?" asked Leon.

"It's beautiful," said Tracy.

"Can you believe that it was night when I first came here, and I took a wrong turn? But when I found this, I realised it was worth it," said Leon.

"You want a better view?" asked Leon as he started getting out of the car.

"Come on," said Leon as he closed the door. Tracy was uncertain, but she got out of the car, too.

For a moment, Tracy couldn't see Leon until she looked up and found him sitting on the roof of the car.

"Come on up," said Leon as he extended his hand. Tracy took his hand and climbed up, then sat on the roof with him.

Leon laid back on the roof as Tracy then did the same. The both of them stared up at the star-filled night sky. A truly beautiful sight that was often only seen in pictures.

"You ever seen a night like this?" asked Leon.

"Once, on a fishing trip with my dad, it was the first time we'd gone night fishing. We didn't catch anything, but that was probably because we spent most of the time staring up at the stars," said Tracy.

"Stars are what make the universe whole, and what lies beyond them is anyone's guess." That's what he told me that night", said Tracy.

"He sounds like a decent man, your dad," said Leon.

"He was," said Tracy with some sadness.

"Did something happen to him?" asked Leon.

"He left, walked out on me and my mom nearly four years ago. Cut off all contact, and we haven't heard from him since," said Tracy.

"Why did he leave?" asked Leon.

"Something happened to me that I don't like to talk about. After it was over, thanks to Jim, who saved me, my parents fought all the time. Mom accused Dad of not being able to protect me, and Dad called Mom a control freak who wasn't letting me have my freedom," said Tracy.

"Then, one day, I came home from school and found mom crying in the kitchen; she'd found a letter my dad had written for us. It said he was leaving, so he'd packed his bags and just…left," said Tracy.

"Jim tracked him down at one point after mom hired him to do so. She found out Dad was refusing to pay any further alimony or child support, so she asked Jim to convince him otherwise, and he did. We all had a sit-down, signed the papers, and that was the very last time we saw him," said Tracy.

"So, is that why Jim is so protective of you?" asked Leon.

"(chuckles) Jim means well; he's a good man, and a lot of people in town respect him for what he does. After that last meeting, he kinda took on the role of my guardian angel. And honestly, I hate the times I resented his help. In some ways.... it would be kinda cool if he was my dad," said Tracy.

"Well, you're lucky to have someone who cares about you, unlike my parents," said Leon.

"I'm sure that's not true, Leon," said Tracy.

"No, it is; everyone thinks because I'm a rich kid who's spoiled rotten that I have the best life. But the truth is that my parents are always working, we never even hang out anymore, they don't even notice I'm there," said Leon.

"Even family dinners are either filled with silence or talking about things that don't make any sense to me. That's half the reason I came down here, to get away from it all," said Leon.

"You know, I called my parents' lawyer when the Sheriff arrested me. I wasn't trying to get out of it, not really. I asked him to put my parents on the line; even if they'd just scold me, at least we'd be talking. But they wouldn't come to the phone; our lawyer just threatened the Sheriff to release me, and that was that," said Leon.

"I'm so sorry, Leon. Not just for your parents, but for the way I treated you," said Tracy.

"Don't apologise, Tracy. You had everything right. I'm sorry I got you into so much trouble. You've been the only person who's been nice to me since I arrived; I'm really glad to have met you," said Leon.

"Me too," said Tracy.

People have often said that the stars inspire romance, which is exactly what happened as Leon leaned over and kissed Tracy.

"Sorry," said Leon.

"I'm not," said Tracy as she smiled.

Leon leaned in again as the two of them started making out. Romance can be found in the strangest places.

Chapter 6
Last Seen Alive

Jim Gold's House: Evening 11:15 pm

Jim was in his bed, trying to get some sleep. But once again, he was being plagued by nightmares; most were surrounding why he left the FBI after something tragic had happened. Jim tossed and turned as he could hear the voices in his head speak.

"It's going to be great," said a woman's voice.

"It sure will be," said Jim's voice.

"You can't be serious!" said Jim's voice.

"It's one job, she'll be well taken care of," said another man's voice.

"Honey, I'll be fine, this has to be done," said the woman's voice.

"Jim, he knows I'm compromised!" said the woman's voice.

"Get out of there!" said Jim's voice.

A loud gunshot followed with the woman's voice screaming.

"NO!!!" screamed Jim's voice as he finally woke up.

He rubbed his face as he was sweating immensely. No matter how hard he tried, the nightmare wouldn't leave him. Because, for the most part, he couldn't let the past go.

The Back Roads of Pike County: 11:21 pm

Leon's car was speeding down the road, but not in the direction of Milford, the car's engine revved loudly as though it was in a race. Leon and Tracy kept giving each other looks; the kissing was as far as it went, but the both of them were hyped up and giddy.

"Shall I show you what she can do?" asked Leon in a suave manner.

"Show me," said Tracy with a smile.

Leon put his foot down as the car's speed revved up to 65 mph. Those kinds of speeds were not built for these types of roads, but Leon didn't care; it was his car, he knew what he was doing.

Tracy let out a loud "WHOOOO!!!" as Leon did the same "WHOOOOO!!".

"Free spirit, eat your heart out!" said Leon with a laugh.

Suddenly, the laughter died down when the sound of a siren cut through, and a police car appeared in the rearview mirror.

"Oh, no, no, no, no, no, no, no, no, no," said Leon.

"Oh, you've got to be kidding me!" said Tracy.

"Relax, Tracy, everything is going to be okay," said Leon.

"OKAY?! That cop wants us to pull over, and the moment we do, he's going to be taking me home in cuffs. Oh my god, mom's going to go mental, and Jim's going to be angry with me and…." Tracy couldn't finish; she was paralysed with fear.

"Just relax, this is my car, remember, I know what I'm doing!" said Leon as he slammed his foot down and put on even more speed than before. The cop car was starting to lag behind.

"See, I told you, these cop cars won't keep up with a model like mine. We'll be home free before you know it," said Leon.

"What about the licence plate?!" asked Tracy.

"Actually, the car is still registered to my father. He bought it for me, but I never changed the ownership," said Leon.

"Dear god, I'm in a car with a madman," said Tracy.

"Look, relax. That cop is barely keeping up with us; points for trying, but we'll soon be (BANG)." Leon was cut off as a loud bang went off and hit the back windshield; it cracked slightly.

"OH MY GOD, is he shooting at us?!!" shouted Tracy as another two loud bangs went off.

"What's this guy's deal?!" said Leon.

Tracy was more terrified than anything. Leon then spotted a side road coming up.

"Hang on," said Leon.

"You mean more than I am now?!" said Tracy.

Leon made a sharp turn onto the side road and drove down it; the cop car followed. Leon kept his eyes open for more turns and took them sharply as well, trying to confuse and eventually lose the cop car. After a number of more turns, Leon finally made it back onto the main road and started speeding up again; the cop car wasn't behind them anymore.

"You see, I told you, you gotta trust the driver," said Leon with a laugh.

Tracy was still frightened, but she managed a small, relieved smile. Then the smile dropped as she looked to her right.

"LEON!!!" shouted Tracy as the cop car suddenly came out of nowhere and rammed into them.

Everything slowed down as Leon's car spun through the air, then rolled down an embankment next to the road and finally came to a standstill at the bottom. The back wheels were still spinning slightly as the car had landed upside down. Leon and Tracy both lay still; they'd miraculously survived the crash but were both unconscious. A flashlight appeared as someone shined a torch into the car.

"Well, well, what do we have here?" said Frank.

Jim Gold's House: Morning 7:00 am

Jim opened his eyes as he'd woken up from another uneasy sleep. He felt tired, but he knew it was time to get up. Jim pulled himself from bed, did his normal bathroom routine, then put some clothes on and came downstairs. He turned on the coffee maker to make himself a cup before figuring out what to do today; he'd either work on a case or check with the Sheriff to see if anything was available. On the one hand, he still had the case of Todd Hunter's missing nest egg, but until the results had come back, there wasn't much else he could do. On the other hand, he was thinking about whether or not to investigate more of Leon's background, to find out the kind of guy he was or if his parents really knew that he was in Milford.

Jim's thoughts were interrupted by a frantic banging on the front door and the pressing of his bell multiple times. He went to the door and opened it; Joey was there, breathing heavily as though he'd been on a marathon.

"Jim…..it's….it's uh…ahhhh…." said Joey, breathlessly.

"Joey, what is it? Why do you look like you're having a heart attack?" asked Jim.

"Sorry….it's my fault…..I ran here from…..the station…..should have taken…..car…..but had to…..come here…..to….." said Joey, still breathless.

"Joey, just breathe, okay, slow and deep. Now, when you're ready, tell me what's wrong," said Jim.

Joey breathed in and out a few times before he answered.

"Miss Kean called the Sheriff this morning to file a missing person report; she says Tracy's disappeared," said Joey.

Tracy Kean's House: Morning 7:07 am

Shortly after pulling himself together from the shock, Jim grabbed his notebook and drove to Tracy's house in his car; he gave Joey a lift, too. He pulled up outside, got out and made his way into the house. A number of deputies were already inside, going around collecting whatever evidence connected to Tracy, as well as fingerprints and DNA samples. Sheriff Hanson was inside the hall, talking to Min and another deputy, Dom Thomas, the average American.

"Okay, Min, you supervise evidence gathering on the ground floor. Dom, you take it upstairs, and I'll handle it outside. Look for anything that might suggest if this is a runaway case or a possible kidnapping; alright, get to it," said Sheriff Hanson as Min and Dom both nodded and went off to carry out their tasks.

Jim went inside as the Sheriff turned and saw him.

"Sheriff, what happened?" asked Jim.

"Now, before I say anything, Jim, I want you to promise me that you'll remain calm and open-minded," said Sheriff Hanson.

"I'm calm, Sheriff, I'm perfectly calm, and I'm always open-minded," said Jim as Joey came in, still a bit breathless.

"Joey, why do you look like you've run a marathon?" asked Sheriff Hanson.

"Well, I ran…to Jim's house…pretty fast," said Joey.

"You could have taken your car if you hadn't charged off like Usain Bolt," said Sheriff Hanson.

"I appreciate the compliment," said Joey as he nearly fell down; Jim stopped him.

"Go sit down before you fall down," said Sheriff Hanson as Joey went to take a seat in the living room.

"Now, Sheriff, what happened here?" asked Jim.

"I only know what Miss Kean told me over the phone. She went up to Tracy's room and found the door was locked. She knocked several times, and when no one answered, she asked a neighbour to climb a ladder and check through her bedroom window. When he said there was no one in there, she phoned the station and said that Tracy was missing," said Sheriff Hanson.

"What else did she say?" asked Jim.

"Not much, she was quite frantic over the phone. I told her to take some time to cool off, and I'd come round personally to take her statement. The deputies are searching the house, as you can see. But Jim, one thing I want you to know, so far there's no sign of a struggle or a break-in. Could it be possible that Tracy left of her own accord? She's done it before," said Sheriff Hanson.

"No, not for the last few years, she wouldn't; she was getting better," said Jim.

"By the way, Jim, as you were one of the last people to see Tracy, I'll need to take your statement too," said Sheriff Hanson.

"Of course," said Jim.

"Okay, I'm going to talk to Miss Kean; you can join me if you like", said Sheriff Hanson as Jim nodded and followed him to the living room where Miss Kean was sitting down.

"I don't understand how this could happen," said Miss Kean, drying her eyes with a tissue. Jim and Sheriff Hanson sat opposite her.

"Miss Kean, can you describe the last evening with Tracy? How was she? Anything bothering her?" asked Sheriff Hanson.

"No, no, everything was fine. We had a nice evening dinner, and she even washed all the dishes; she's good at that. Most people like her hate chores, but she actually likes doing them. And I don't think anything was bothering her; she seemed her normal self," said Miss Kean.

"How about locking her room? Does Tracy normally do that?" asked Sheriff Hanson.

"Oh, she insisted on getting that lock herself, didn't want me barging in her "private space". You know what kids her age are like, all-girl power magazines and pictures of cute boys", said Miss Kean.

"Did you see or hear anything strange last night?" asked Sheriff Hanson.

"No, not that I can recall; it was a normal evening. Tracy was her usual self, and aside from the odd car going by, no, nothing strange," said Miss Kean.

"Um, if I can interject for a moment. Miss Kean, last night Tracy expressed some…concern for your health; she said you'd been struggling recently," said Jim.

"Oh, I've just had a few bad months, that's all; that girl worries too much. Did you see Tracy last night? She's always wandering off that girl," said Miss Kean.

"Miss Kean, I walked Tracy home; remember, we talked briefly on the front doorstep," said Jim.

"We did?" said Miss Kean as she seemed to zone out for a second.

"Oh yes, we did, you're right. Oh, it was so good of you to bring her home. That girl is always wandering off; I never know what she's doing half the time," said Miss Kean.

Jim and Sheriff Hanson looked at each other.

"Miss Kean, can you think of any reason why Tracy might want to run away?" asked Sheriff Hanson.

"No, no, of course not. I can't think of any reason why she'd leave without telling me," said Miss Kean.

"Oh, this is going to be so difficult to explain when her father gets home," said Miss Kean.

Sheriff Hanson and Jim looked at each other again.

After concluding the interview, Jim, Sheriff Hanson and Joey convened in the hallway.

"Well, guys, I'm not one to theorise, but I don't think Miss Kean is all that well," said Joey.

"I'm no doctor, but I think she may be exhibiting the symptoms of early onset dementia," said Sheriff Hanson.

"I also think something's wrong with her statement," said Jim.

"You think she's lying?" asked Joey.

"I wouldn't say that; she's just not being entirely truthful with us," said Jim.

"Well, we should get Doctor Mcallister to give her a check-up," said Joey.

"You're right; I'll give him a call. In the meantime, Jim, I'm still going to need you to come to the station and give your statement," said Sheriff Hanson.

"Of course, Sheriff, but there's one thing I need to do first," said Jim.

"What?" asked Sheriff Hanson.

"I need to look in Tracy's room....to satisfy a curiosity," said Jim.

"Well…okay, go ahead. Joey, go with him," said Sheriff Hanson.

"It's okay, I need to do this alone; I'll be back in a minute", said Jim as he went up the stairs.

Joey and Sheriff Hanson looked at each other, wondering what was going through Jim's mind.

Jim entered Tracy's room as a deputy left after finishing his evidence gathering. He just took a moment to look around; Tracy's room wasn't like Miss Kean described, not as girly anyway. Jim then noticed the picture of him and Tracy in their fishing gear; he picked up the picture and closed his eyes.

He remembered being in the fishing boat with Tracy on the lake, their rods in the water and waiting for the fish.

"They're not biting as much today," said Tracy.

"And your dad thought this was a fun activity?" said Jim as Tracy laughed.

"They're usually more active than this," said Tracy.

"You know, my dad once told me that a way to get the fish's attention was to stick your bare feet into the water, and the fish nibble your toes," said Tracy.

"You're more than welcome to do that; I have no intention of letting my feet be nibbled by fish the size of mice," said Jim.

"Jim, I don't think I said thank you properly, I mean. I know that you're bored out of your mind, but it was still nice of you to try," said Tracy.

"It's my pleasure, Tracy, though maybe we could pick another activity next time. Like, I don't know, go-karting," said Jim as both he and Tracy laughed.

The laughter faded as Jim came back to the real world. He put the picture back down and left Tracy's room.

Chapter 7
The Investigation Begins

Milford Sheriff's Department: Morning, 8:09 am

Jim was now sitting in one of the interview rooms in the Sheriff's department; Sheriff Hanson sat opposite him.

"Okay, Jim, I talked to Shaw last night, and he gave me the rundown of what occurred in the bar. Then Joey filled me in on the fight in the alley. Nice work, by the way," said Sheriff Hanson. Jim smirked.

"But everything that happened after you left with Tracy was seen with your eyes only. So, walk me through it," said Sheriff Hanson.

"There's not much to tell. I walked Tracy home, we talked about things, I covered for her when Miss Kean questioned where she was, Tracy gave me a hug, and then I left," said Jim.

"During the interview, you said that Tracy told you she was concerned about her mother's health," said Sheriff Hanson.

"I gently cautioned Tracy for calling her mother a control freak. She then told me during the walk that her mother was forgetting things, getting angry over the small stuff and not noticing her a lot of the time or what she did around the house," said Jim.

"You said that you didn't think Miss Kean was being truthful to us. Could she have done something that caused Tracy to run away?" said Sheriff Hanson.

"Maybe, but without proof, I can only theorise that," said Jim.

"I'm sorry, Sheriff, but there really isn't anything more to say. I walked Tracy home, and we talked; I know I spoke to her mother briefly, and then I gave Tracy my card and said to call me if she needed anything. That was the last time I saw her," said Jim.

"Okay, well, thanks anyway, Jim, every bit helps", said Sheriff Hanson as he and Jim got up, then left the room and entered the main area.

"Sheriff!" suddenly said Joey as he and Min came running over.

"Sheriff, I just had a thought. Leon Thornberg, you released him last night," said Joey.

"Oh Christ, I can't believe I forgot that," said Sheriff Hanson.

"What if Leon went looking for Tracy, trying to get back into her good books?" asked Joey.

"Then, if something did happen at the house that caused Tracy to leave, Leon must have found her walking the street," said Jim.

"But did she go with him willingly, or did he kidnap her?" asked Min.

"If that goddamn city boy is behind this….." said Sheriff Hanson.

"Alright, Jim, I'm officially hiring you as Sheriff of Milford. If Leon is behind Tracy's disappearance, then we're going to need your help to track this son of a bitch down and bring her home," said Sheriff Hanson.

"You can count on me, Sheriff" said Jim.

"I was hoping you'd say that," said Sheriff Hanson with a smile.

"So where do we start? I mean, the only way Leon could have gotten Tracy out of Milford was with a car, and I don't know if he even had one," said Joey.

"Oh, he has a car, all right; I remember he was bragging about it while his lawyer had me on hold," said Sheriff Hanson.

"We could check the traffic cameras by the town exits to see if a car registered to Leon came through any of them," said Min.

"That's a good idea, Min. Get what footage you can from last night. I know I tried to block Leon out at one point, but he said something about his car being capable of running a race if that helps," said Sheriff Hanson.

"Thanks, Sheriff, I'm on it," said Min as she walked away to carry out her task.

"If only we had some way of telling where Tracy was last night and if she was picked up by Leon. A witness would be good, but there are so few people walking the streets at night," said Joey.

"I don't think we can waste our time questioning every resident in town," said Jim.

"Maybe we won't have to; I have an idea," said Sheriff Hanson.

"What's that?" asked Joey.

"The power of the Violet Show," said Sheriff Hanson.

1 Hour Later

A playlist was heard over the radio until it was stopped abruptly.

"Greetings, residents of Milford; this is Violet, host of the Violet Show. I apologise for interrupting your morning playlist, but I have an important announcement to make," said Violet over the radio.

"As the news may have spread around town, Tracy Kean, a born and raised resident and a good friend of mine and Eileen's, has disappeared. She went missing after leaving her home last night," said Violet.

"The Sheriff's department has a suspect, a city boy named Leon Thornberg, who recently arrived. Apparently, he's a spoiled rich kid who showed an interest in Tracy, and after an incident I wasn't told of, she gave him his marching orders," said Violet.

"My uncle has asked me to give an appeal to you, the residents of Milford. If anyone happened to be going for a late night stroll or looked out their window into the street, and you saw either Tracy or Leon, then I ask that you please come forward and inform the Sheriff or Jim Gold," said Violet.

"If Leon thinks he can just snatch someone and we won't care, he's wrong. We look out for one another in this town; we're a family, and only by working together can we find Tracy and bring her safely home," said Violet.

"And yes, we're still holding out hope for the safe return of Derek Johnson and the others who were with him two nights ago. Thank you, everyone; I'll see you all later for the afternoon edition," said Violet as she closed her microphone and signalled Eileen to resume the playlist.

Somewhere in the Pike County Wilderness

Back at the unknown property in the Pike County Wilderness, Tracy was lying in the same barn where Cassie, Tammy and Jimmy were being held. The three of them had been trying to wake her and Leon up. Finally, they both started to regain consciousness.

"She's waking up, Tracy, Tracy, can you hear me? It's Cassie!" said Cassie as Tracy opened her eyes and groaned.

"Careful, don't move too quickly", said Cassie as Tracy was now awake and realised who was talking to her.

"Cassie, Cassie!" said Tracy as she hugged her; Cassie hugged back.

"I didn't know if you were alive; I was so worried that…." Tracy couldn't finish.

"I was starting to think the same of you for a moment," said Cassie.

Tracy then noticed the others.

"Tammy?" said Tracy as they hugged.

"It's good to see you, Tracy. Not exactly glad you're here, but it's good to see you all the same," said Tammy.

"Jimmy, what happened to you?" asked Tracy as Jimmy had a few more cuts and bruises than before.

"A little worse for wear, and yes, it still hurts," said Jimmy as Tracy hugged him.

"I'm so glad you guys are alive. The Sheriff's Department has been trying to find you, but there is only so much they can do. Wait, where's Derek?" said Tracy as everyone looked at each other.

"We got pulled over by these county cops; they accused us of clipping a deer because we were driving under the influence. They cuffed the three of us and put us in their car, but after they cuffed Derek….one of the cops pulled a gun and aimed it at him….Derek tried to run……and the cop fucking shot him!" said Jimmy with tears in his eyes. Tracy felt the same as the shock hit her hard like a thunderbolt.

"Oh my god, Jimmy, I'm so sorry", said Tracy.

Leon started to wake up.

"So, how did you end up here, Tracy?" asked Cassie.

"Well, that's all thanks to this idiot," said Tracy.

"Oh, come on, babe, I thought we'd mended things," said Leon.

"Yeah, that was before you broke the speed limit and got us chased by a psycho cop who takes his job way too seriously!" said Tracy.

"Wait, what happened, and who is this anyway?" asked Jimmy.

"Leon Thornberg. I took Tracy here for a drive in my car; I may have gone slightly over the speed limit. Next thing we know, some cop is chasing us, then shooting at us, and just when I thought we'd lost him, he comes out of nowhere and rams my car off the goddamn road!" said Leon.

"That guy better watch out. Once I get his badge number, I'm suing his ass for the damages," said Leon.

Everyone looked at each other.

"Yeah, I don't think you get the full ramifications of what's happening here, buddy," said Jimmy.

"Where are we?" asked Tracy.

"We don't know, some kind of barn. There's an older guy and his son here, both with redneck accents; his son's is slightly stronger. They come in, taunt us a bit, then they drag us into this farmhouse across the way and….have fun with us," said Cassie.

"What do you mean by fun?" asked Leon.

"Well, for the most part, they hit us, cut us, laugh at us and make insulting comments about what horrible people we are," said Jimmy.

"The older guy said we each get three chances; if we lose them…they promise that they'll kill us," said Cassie.

"Well, I don't feel like waiting around for that to happen. There has to be a way out of here. Have you guys tried to come up with an escape plan?" said Tracy.

"Well…we have a plan, but it's more suicide than escape," said Tammy.

"What?" asked Tracy.

"Jimmy here wants to take on the cops who kidnapped us," said Tammy.

"Hey, I've narrowed it down to the cop who shot Derek!" said Jimmy.

"Alright, guys, I know things seem hopeless at the moment, but I think if we keep calm and stay together, we'll find a way out of here. And no matter what happens, we won't let those guys break us, agreed?" said Tracy as everyone slightly smiled and nodded.

Suddenly, there was the sound of the barn door being unlocked.

"They're coming. Whatever happens, don't make any moves against them; they're not as stupid as they look," said Cassie.

Harlan and Cletus entered the barn. Cletus aimed his shotgun at Cassie, Tammy and Jimmy as the three of them backed up slowly with their hands slightly raised. Harlan approached Leon and Tracy.

"So, I thought it was best to introduce ourselves to the new arrivals. Welcome to…the Barn," said Harlan with a slight laugh.

Leon suddenly got up.

"Okay, you listen to me, you yokel trash!" said Leon.

"Oh boy, here we go," said Jimmy.

"I don't think you and your son know exactly who you're dealing with!" said Leon.

"Well then, why don't you indulge us?" said Harlan.

"My name is Leon Thornberg; my family is among the richest and most powerful in New York City. They know cops, lawyers, and even members of the Federal Bureau. If they don't hear from me soon, they'll send the FBI down here to find me, and you and your son will go to federal prison or an asylum. So it's in your best interests if you let me go," said Leon.

Harlan seemed to think about it for a moment. Then he and Cletus burst out laughing.

"He's even stupider than that guy, Pa," said Cletus.

"Oh, thank you Mr Thornberg, it's been a while since me and the boy have had a good laugh. Now, as it happens, I know who you are, Leon. I checked your wallet (he shows Leon's wallet in his hand)," said Harlan.

"So if your parents are as rich as you say, then maybe we can strike some kind of deal," said Harlan.

"I thought you said this wasn't about the money," said Cassie.

"Oh, it isn't. But then again, you're not exactly rich; he is," said Harlan.

"Why don't we go into the farmhouse and discuss it?" said Harlan as he grabbed Leon by the back of his head and dragged him out of the barn while he protested. Cletus followed while still aiming his shotgun back and forth at everyone, then the doors closed and locked.

"So, how certain are you that we're going to get out of here?" asked Cassie.

"I'm certain. And even if we can't, there's someone out there who'll move heaven and earth to find us. I know he will," said

Tracy with confidence; she knew who she meant and hoped that she was right.

Chapter 8
Deep Pains

Milford Sheriff's Department: Morning 10:15 am

The town was abuzz with the story of Tracy's disappearance and the possible connection to Leon Thornberg; some people were even crying out for his blood. So far, since Violet's broadcast, no one had come forward, but Sheriff Hanson wasn't willing to wait. Both he and Jim had decided to interrogate the thugs that threatened Leon last night to try and get a feel of the kind of person he was.

Sheriff Hanson and Jim sat in the interview room with one of the thugs, his name was Simon, on the opposite side.

"Okay, now then, Simon, is it? I want to get your version of last night, but I believe there's something you really want to tell me?" said Sheriff Hanson.

"Yeah, I want to file charges against him (points at Jim); he assaulted me and my boys viciously and unfairly," said Simon.

"Well, from my understanding, you pulled an unlicensed firearm on one of my deputies, manhandled and threatened a resident of Milford, then you and your boys attacked this man (points at Jim), which gave him every right to defend himself. So if you'd like to make this official, then go ahead; I'll even give you a phone," said Sheriff Hanson.

Simon seemed to be deflated and not so eager anymore.

"I thought so, now down to business. What did you want with Leon Thornberg last night?" said Sheriff Hanson.

"We just wanted to discuss some business with him; we heard he was in town and decided to talk to him," said Simon.

"You just so happened to be passing through town despite the fact that the background checks show you and your boys all have permanent residences in New York?" said Sheriff Hanson.

"We were just on a little holiday, taking in the sights," said Simon.

"You must think we're really stupid, Simon. I heard what you said, and Leon confirmed it; he said he owes you money. Is that true?" said Jim.

"You can't believe a word that kid says; he'd say anything to get out of trouble," said Simon.

"And you're not getting out of trouble here either. I know you think you can spin some story of innocence and that we'll believe it, but Jim's right; we're not that stupid," said Sheriff Hanson.

"Now start telling us the truth, or else I'll also be charging you in connection to Leon's sudden disappearance", said Sheriff Hanson as Simon's eyes widened.

"What are you talking about?" asked Simon.

"Leon Thornberg hasn't been seen since last night. It's also suspected he's behind the kidnapping of a local girl, Tracy Kean, who one of your boys pinned to the wall in the alley," said Jim.

"We....we don't have anything to do with that. Besides, we've been locked in a cell all night!" said Simon.

"You don't expect us to believe that there aren't more of you, especially if money is concerned. Leon could have attempted to leave Milford after taking Tracy, in which case you had backup waiting. If he tried, then they did away with him. So the question remains, what happened to Tracy?" said Jim.

"NO, no, you've got it all wrong; there's no one else. It's just us four, we didn't do anything to him or his girlfriend, I swear!" said Simon.

"Then help us understand, how much did Simon owe you?" said Jim.

"He....Leon didn't technically owe us anything, but his parents did," said Simon.

"Go on," said Sheriff Hanson.

"There's this architect back in New York. The Thorbergs have been getting into construction, and they hired this guy to draw out their plans," said Simon.

"What have they built?" asked Jim.

"Few fancy hotels, some restaurants, the architect is quite good with his planning, and he takes safety very seriously", said Simon.

"So what went wrong?" asked Sheriff Hanson.

"The last construction, the Thornbergs refused to pay him. They accused him of cutting corners and said that certain safety requirements hadn't been met," said Simon.

"But they were met, and the family was just skimming his payment," said Jim.

"Pretty much; the architect then hired us to track down the son, Leon. He couldn't go after the Thornbergs without them calling the police, but he thought if we could get to their son and either reason with or threaten him, maybe they'd pay up," said Simon.

"Thank you, Simon, we've got what we need," said Sheriff Hanson as he and Jim got up.

"So, I did good, right?" asked Simon.

"Yes, you did," said Sheriff Hanson.

"Oh good," said Simon.

"I'm still charging you, though," said Sheriff Hanson as he and Jim left the room.

"Wait, wait a minute (Simon gets up and starts banging on the door); I gave you guys information; you have to take the charges off, or at least shorten the sentence. Come on man, be fair, I can't go to prison, my mom says I'm too soft, come on, have a heart!!" shouted Simon through the door.

"I love the sound of hopeless begging in the morning", said Sheriff Hanson as he and Jim laughed a bit.

"Sheriff", suddenly said Dom as he ran up to them.

"What is it, Dom?" asked Sheriff Hanson.

"Gomez and his mother, Miss Salazer, are here; he says he's coming forward with information about Tracy," said Dom.

"Where are they now?" asked Jim.

"Just by the entrance," said Dom.

"Okay, thank you, Dom. Can you move Simon back to the cells after he's cooled off?" said Sheriff Hanson.

"Sure thing, Sheriff; how long should I wait?" said Dom as Simon started banging on the door loudly again and shouting incoherently.

"Might want to make it an hour", said Jim as he and Sheriff Hanson walked away.

They went to the main entrance where Gomez and his mother were waiting with Deputy Brandon.

"Gomez, Miss Salazar," said Sheriff Hanson.

"Hello, Sheriff, Jim," said Gomez.

"Hey Gomez, we understand you're coming forward about Tracy," said Jim.

"I am, yes, I heard the broadcast on the Violet Show. I'm sorry I didn't come sooner, but I've been looking after my mother," said Gomez.

"You okay, Miss Salazar?" asked Sheriff Hanson.

"I'm fine, Sheriff; I've just had a bad morning. Thank the Lord my son was there," said Miss Salazar.

"Okay, Gomez, whatever you have to tell us about Tracy, start from the beginning and don't leave out any details", said Jim.

"Okay, so last night I was working the night shift at the General Store," said Gomez. He was Todd Hunter's one and only employee at the store.

"The General Store has a night shift?" asked Joey.

"It's something new Mr Hunter is trying; he only started it about a week ago. I don't think it's going to catch on, though; who wants to shop at 1:00 am, right?" said Gomez.

"1:00 am? I don't think he pays you enough, Gomez," said Joey as he and Gomez laughed.

"Um, sorry, anyway, I was in the store; it was roughly 10:11 pm, no one had come in, so I was just doing some sweeping up. I stopped for a moment, and when I looked out the front, I saw Tracy walking on the other side of the street," said Gomez.

"How did she seem?" asked Jim.

"Well, I know it was from a distance, but she looked sad. And the left side of her face, bearing in mind I couldn't really tell, looked a little blue like it was bruised or something," said Gomez.

"What happened next?" asked Sheriff Hanson.

"Well, I finally decided to go out and see if she was okay. But before I got out the door, this yellow racing car came out of nowhere and started driving next to her," said Gomez.

"Did you see the driver?" asked Sheriff Hanson.

"No, sorry, he was too fast, and I was at the wrong angle to see," said Gomez.

"Okay, go on," said Jim.

"Well, I stayed by the entrance and watched the car follow Tracy for a bit, then it stopped as she did. She seemed to talk to whoever the driver was for a while, then she got in the car, and it drove away really fast," said Gomez.

"Did she get into the car forcefully or willingly?" asked Jim.

Gomez seemed unsure he wanted to answer; his mother touched his arm and smiled.

"Willingly, she got in willingly," said Gomez.

Jim rubbed his head a bit and sighed.

"You didn't happen to see anything else last night?" asked Sheriff Hanson.

"Actually, yes. Before the car drove away, I found some paper and quickly wrote down the licence plate. I have it here," said Gomez as he handed the piece of paper to Sheriff Hanson.

"Joey, run these plates as quickly as you can," said Sheriff Hanson.

"Yes, Sheriff," said Joey as he walked away to carry out the task.

"You've been very helpful, Gomez; you should be proud of yourself," said Jim.

"Thank you," said Gomez as he started leading his mother out.

"Mr Gold, I hope you find Tracy. She's one of the good ones," said Gomez.

"Yes, she is," said Jim as Gomez and his mother left the station.

"You okay?" asked Sheriff Hanson.

"Why wouldn't I be?" said Jim.

"Well, you reacted when you heard Tracy get into the car willingly," said Sheriff Hanson.

"It's….it's not something she'd do. I saw Tracy verbally rebuke Leon in the alley, and then, not even an hour or so later, she got into a car with the guy. Something's wrong," said Jim.

"Sheriff, Jim, I think I have something", said Min as she directed the two of them to her desk and showed them the screen of her computer, an older model that didn't get many updates.

"I've been reviewing the traffic camera footage from last night, and I found this at the West side town exit", said Min as she played the footage and stopped it when a car appeared on the screen.

"A yellow racing car, just like Gomez said," said Sheriff Hanson.

"Can we get an angle on the driver?" asked Jim.

"I'm afraid not, but we can get an angle on the passenger seat," said Min as she changed cameras and showed the passenger seat of the car from the side. The unmistakable face and blonde hair colour of Tracy was there, she was looking out the window to her right.

"So she is in the car," said Jim.

"Well, we don't know if it was willingly. Leon could have restrained her after she got in," said Sheriff Hanson.

"I don't know, from this angle, she doesn't look like a scared hostage," said Min.

"Got the plates back," said Joey as he came over.

"Does the car belong to Leon?" asked Jim.

"Actually, it's a little complicated. Leon is the licensed driver of the car, but its registration belongs to his father," said Joey.

"Well, that's hardly surprising. What better way to get out of paying parking fines and speeding tickets than to send them all to Daddy?" said Sheriff Hanson.

Joey looked at the screen.

"Oh, so Tracy is in the car," said Joey.

Jim leaned in for a closer look at the screen.

"What is it?" asked Min.

"Gomez said the left side of Tracy's face looked blue like it was bruised. You can just about make something out. Can we clear up this image a bit more?" said Jim.

"Not with the technology we have. We could do it manually, but that'll take hours," said Min as Jim reached for his phone and dialled a number.

"Who are you calling?" asked Joey.

"An old friend who may be able to help us," said Jim as he put the phone to his ear.

The call went long distance to the FBI building in Washington, DC. The person Jim was calling was Special Agent Dylan Ross, one of his friends he kept in touch with. Dylan was about 30ish with slightly long hair. He knew people called him a hippie behind his back, but he didn't care for their comments and always just brushed them off. Dylan was playing games on his computer in the office; it was a slow work day. His phone was on the desk when it rang; the ringtone was the song Don't Stop Me Now. Dylan picked up the phone and smiled as he saw the name; he pressed to answer.

"Jimmy, my buddy, how are you?" said Dylan with a happy attitude

"I'm doing good, Dylan; how's tricks?" said Jim.

"Oh, you know, it's all get-up and go here. Busy one minute, busy the next, non-stop action!" said Dylan.

"So, how's the game going?" said Jim as Dylan laughed a bit.

"Okay, okay, you got me. It's actually going pretty well; just one more quest and I get the Cape of Good Fortune," said Dylan. The game he was playing was World Of Warcraft.

"So, is it business or pleasure?" asked Dylan.

"I'm sorry to say, but it's business, Dylan. There's something I could really use your help with," said Jim.

"Sure thing, buddy; how can I help?" said Dylan.

"We've just had a kidnapping, a 23-year-old girl named Tracy Kean. Our main suspect is a guy named Leon Thornberg," said Jim.

"Oh, that's horrible, that poor girl. Listen, Jim, I'm familiar with the Thornbergs; they're powerful people and not the sort you want to mess with. They can make your life a misery if you do," said Dylan.

"Well, thankfully, I don't have any plans to upset them. But here's the thing, Dylan, we have an image from a traffic camera that's important to the investigation. If we email it to you, could you clear it up for us?" said Jim.

"Of course, buddy, send it over, and I'll see what I can do", said Dylan as Jim had been preparing the email amidst the call; he then pressed send. It came through as Dylan looked at the attached image.

"Should be a piece of cake; just give me two minutes", said Dylan as he started to work his magic.

"So Dylan is one of your friends?" asked Joey.

"Oh yeah, Dylan and I were partners for a while; we worked together on a number of cases. Then, he got promoted with his own office and was pulled from fieldwork. He's still a good guy, though, and a wizard with computers," said Jim.

"Okay, Jim, are you still there?" asked Dylan.

"Yeah, I'm here," said Jim.

"I've done what I can to clear up the image; it looks a little better anyway. I'm sending it back in the reply," said Dylan as the email came back to Min's computer.

She opened the image, and it was a lot clearer than last time.

"You're amazing, Dylan, thanks so much," said Jim.

"Anytime, buddy, you let me know if I can help more in any way," said Dylan.

"Appreciate it, buddy, talk to you soon, bye," said Jim as he ended the call and put the phone away.

Everyone was looking at the image; they could now see the bruise on Tracy's face.

"Did he hit her?" asked Joey.

"If he did, I swear to god…" said Jim.

"Sheriff," said a voice as a man in his late sixties approached them.

"Doctor Mcallister," said Sheriff Hanson. Doctor Albert Mcallister was Milford's resident sawbones.

"Did you do a prognosis on Miss Kean?" asked Joey.

"I did, and the Sheriff is right. She's exhibiting all the signs of early onset dementia," said Doctor Mcallister.

"Now, as my medical knowledge only goes so far, she'll still have to be taken to a proper hospital for more tests. Is that Tracy?" said Doctor Mcallister as he noticed the image of Tracy in the car.

"Doctor, can you see that bruise on Tracy's face, left side? Could that be caused by someone hitting her?" asked Jim as Doctor Mcallister put on his reading glasses and took a closer look.

"My god, yes, I'm afraid that bruising is from someone hitting her, and the only reason I know is because I've had my share of abuse victims. I know the signs, blackened around the eye and bright bruising underneath. God, that poor girl," said Doctor Mcallister.

"Can you tell who might have hit her, a man or a woman?" asked Min.

"Not with this image, no, I'd need to see her face to face to do an examination. But I can tell that the progress of the wound means it was recent," said Doctor Mcallister.

A thought suddenly struck in Jim's head; he played back his conversation with Tracy that night. Then it hit him as he walked out of the station.

"Jim, Jim, what is it? Joey, go after him," said Sheriff Hanson as Joey ran to catch up with Jim.

Tracy Kean's House: Morning 10:30 am

Jim had gotten into his car and driven to the Kean house. Joey had followed in his own car.

Jim got out and approached the front door; he didn't look happy. Joey got out, too and followed him.

"Jim, what's happening? Jim, talk to me," said Joey as they reached the front door, and Jim started hammering on it.

"Jim, whatever's going on, we can sort it out without going crazy here," said Joey as Miss Kean opened the door.

"Hello, Jim, Deputy Brandon. To what do I owe the pleasure?" said Miss Kean, who seemed to be in high spirits.

"Did you hit her?" asked Jim.

"What?" asked Miss Kean.

"I asked you a question. Did you hit Tracy?" said Jim.

"Jim, I don't appreciate your tone or the accusations you're making," said Miss Kean.

"This is crossing a line here, buddy," said Joey.

"There's something I didn't tell the Sheriff, mostly because I hoped it wasn't true. Tracy said there'd been some close calls where her mother had nearly hit her but never actually done it. She was adamant that it could never happen!" said Jim.

"You see, I've been wracking my brain, trying to figure out why Tracy would leave the safety of her home and get into a car with someone who I saw her personally rebuke. It didn't make any sense," said Jim.

"Then, after what Doctor Mcallister said, it seemed like it was the only solution. Tracy was attacked by her own mother, that's why she left, that's why she went with Leon, that's why she's missing. Isn't that right, Miss Kean?!" said Jim, getting angry.

"Yes, YES, YOU'RE RIGHT, I HIT HER!!!" suddenly shouted Miss Kean as she burst into tears. Joey went over to comfort her.

"I didn't mean to....you have to believe me...I didn't..." said Miss Kean.

"It's okay, Miss Kean, we know you didn't mean to, don't we, Jim?" said Joey. Jim didn't respond.

"I found these cigarettes in her jacket and....I thought she was smoking again....I questioned her, and things....got out of hand...I didn't even realise I'd hit her. I just turned, and she was standing there with a bruise on her face....I didn't mean to...." said Miss Kean as Jim walked away.

"It's going to be okay, Miss Kean; I'll get Doctor Mcallister to come round again, okay?" said Joey as Miss Kean smiled and nodded a bit. Joey then went after Jim.

"Jim, Jim, I think you owe Miss Kean an apology!" said Joey.

"Why, because she hit her own daughter and drove her into the arms of a delinquent city boy?" said Jim.

"She's not well, Jim, you heard what Doctor Mcallister said. Dementia is a terrible thing; Miss Kean didn't mean to do it; she didn't even realise it'd happened until it was too late," said Joey.

"Look, Jim, I know you care about Tracy, and I know you're worried about her; I am too. But strong-arming her mother isn't going to help matters!" said Joey.

"You're right, of course you're right. I'm sorry, Joey, what am I doing?!" said Jim

"It's just…I never should have left her, I shouldn't have…what the hell kind of guardian angel am I?!" said Jim as he started walking away.

"Jim, Jim!" said Joey, but Jim didn't respond.

He wasn't usually rude and didn't normally shout and upset people; he was a kind person who cared about a person's feelings. But now his attitude was changing; he wanted to find Tracy, and in kidnapping cases, he'd worked in the past, he'd always hated it when people lied to him. It just meant that more time was lost chasing ghosts than finding the victims before it was too late.

Joey considered going after Jim when his radio squawked.

"Deputy Brandon, this is the Sheriff; come in," said Sheriff Hanson.

"I'm here, Sheriff," said Joey.

"Is Jim with you?" asked Sheriff Hanson.

"He's actually walking ahead of me; he's a bit upset," said Joey.

"Well, catch up to him, and then both of you get back to the station. We have a new situation developing," said Sheriff Hanson.

"Oh no, what now?" asked Joey.

"The FBI are here," said Sheriff Hanson.

Chapter 9
Uninvited Guests

Milford Sheriff's Department: Morning 10:40 am

Joey caught up with Jim, and the both of them drove back to the Sheriff's department; they went inside and headed for the main area. They saw the Sheriff talking to an African American man in his fifties and wearing a dark suit. Two other men in suits were standing behind him. Jim recognised the type he'd worn for years in the FBI.

Min and Dom approached them as they came in.

"What's going on?" asked Joey.

"Those guys just showed up about a few minutes after you both left. They identified themselves as FBI agents and wanted to talk to the sheriff," said Dom.

"They've been at it for the last ten minutes. I tried to eavesdrop, but one of them saw me," said Min.

"Great, just what we need, a team of FBI pencil pushers.....oh, no offence, Jim," said Joey.

But Jim wasn't paying attention; he was staring straight ahead at the African-American guy; something in him had been stirred up. The man then noticed Jim and approached him with a smile on his face.

"Jim, Jim Gold? I thought that was you, it's me, Francis Morgan, remember me?" said Francis; Jim didn't respond.

Suddenly, Jim swung his fist and punched Francis in the face; he then started wailing at him with even more punches while he was on the ground; he was really angry.

"Jim!" suddenly said Joey as Jim snapped out of his fantasy.

"Jim, are you okay…..do you know him, the agent?" asked Joey.

"Yeah, you could say that," said Jim as Francis noticed and approached him, this time for real.

"Jim, Jim Gold? I don't believe it, it is you; how are you doing, buddy?" said Francis as he extended his hand. Jim didn't take it.

"It's me, Francis Morgan; we worked together in the FBI, man. Come on, don't tell me you don't remember," said Francis as he retracted his hand.

"Yeah, yeah, I remember you, Francis," said Jim.

"Oh, come on, Jim, you're not still sore about what happened, are you? It was years ago, man, and I told you it wasn't my fault," said Francis. Jim didn't respond.

"Okay, who are you, and what are you doing in our town?" asked Joey.

"Direct and straight to the point, I like it. I'm Special Agent Francis Morgan of the FBI; these two behind me are my colleagues, Thomas Lincoln and Carl Fitzgerald," said Francis.

"We've been sent here at the personal request of the Thornberg Family to locate their son, Leon. Now, apparently, the family's lawyer received a phone call from Leon saying he was in the town of Milford and he wanted to talk to his parents, but they refused to come to the phone. Since then, they've heard nothing, and according to the Sheriff, Leon is missing," said Francis.

"He's not just missing; we suspect he's also behind kidnapping a local girl, Tracy Kean," said Jim.

"Really? Well, that's interesting. Sheriff, when were you planning on telling me this?" said Francis.

"I was about to. Before you cut me off and walked away to play memory lane with your best friend," said Sheriff Hanson.

"He's not my best friend; he's not even my friend," said Jim.

"Damn Jim, that cuts deep," said Francis.

"I was also about to tell you that we've had a number of other disappearances around Pike County. Mostly teenagers, but Tracy and Leon are the most recent to go missing," said Sheriff Hanson.

"Well, I'm sorry to hear that. So look, we're going to be setting up our investigation here in the station, and certain resources will be made available to help us conduct it," said Francis.

"So you're going to help us find out who's behind these disappearances?" asked Min.

"Eeh, sort of. At the moment, there's a possible connection to Leon, so we'll help investigate that matter for the time being. But make no mistake, our priority is Leon Thornberg only," said Francis. Jim scoffed.

"Still the same, eh, Francis, you haven't changed a bit. It's still "The ship's sinking; save the politician and let the rest of them drown", right?" said Jim.

"Look, Jim, you may not agree with my methods but don't question my motives. I understand that every life matters, but sometimes you need to focus on the priorities, especially when those priorities concern the people who control your paycheck," said Francis.

"Now, the Sheriff tells me that despite being a lowly PI, you're actually held in high regard and respected by the townspeople," said Francis.

"I never called Jim a lowly PI!" said Sheriff Hanson.

"No, you didn't, I did," said Francis.

"So Jim, obviously, the FBI isn't liked very much, and I can't afford my investigation to be hampered. Meaning it would be in everyone's best interest if you informed the townspeople that they should be cooperative and open-minded while we're here" said Francis.

"Milford is a free town, Francis, and the people here are free to live as they want. I'd prefer to let them make up their own minds about whether or not they want to cooperate with you," said Jim.

"Now listen, Jim, I understand that you're not FBI anymore and have grown accustomed to doing things your way. But let this be a warning: if you don't help us, if you withhold information or do any investigating without my authority, then I swear, I will reign you in so hard, I will put a collar around your neck and stick you in a kennel like a good dog!" said Francis.

"And that goes the same for the rest of you!" Francis shouted to everyone else in the main area.

"If anyone here does anything to interfere, impede, disrupt or hampen our investigation, then just remember, I have a lot of collars and a lot of kennels!" shouted Francis as Joey suddenly stepped closer to him.

"Now you listen to me, Mr Federal Agent. I know that you guys have some highly superior complex where you work, but Milford is our town; we look out for one another here. So we'll help however we can, but we are going to find our missing people, with or without you. And one more thing, there's only two people in this town who we stand behind and will follow into the fires of hell if necessary: Sheriff Hanson and Jim Gold. They are who we listen to and follow, not you. Are we clear?!" said Joey in a very confident voice.

Francis just stood there for a moment before he smiled.

"I admire your confidence, Deputy, and your statement is duly noted. Now, where can we set up our office?" said Francis.

"We've got a spare room you can use. Dom, can you show them the way?" said Sheriff Hanson as Dom led the agents away. Francis gave a wink as he walked away, Jim didn't react.

"Joey, are you okay?" asked Min.

"I'm fine," said Joey.

"You don't look fine," said Min.

"I can't move my legs," said Joey, revealing he was slightly in shock after standing up to an FBI agent. Jim and Min helped him to sit down.

"That was very brave of you, Joey," said Sheriff Hanson.

"Yeah, all this shaking is me realising that I'm brave," said Joey.

"Sheriff, we're not going to let them do this, are we?" asked Min.

"Shaw's Bar, tonight, 10:30, don't be late", whispered Sheriff Hanson as everyone got the message and went back to it as though everything was normal.

Somewhere in the Pike County Wilderness

At the unknown property, Tracy was staring out the front of the barn through a crack in the wood. She was looking at the farmhouse across the way and the muddied ground all around them.

Leon approached Tracy; he'd been brought back a while ago with a few cuts and bruises, same as the others.

"Hey," said Leon.

"Hey," said Tracy without even looking at him.

"Come on, Tracy, you're not still mad, are you?" said Leon.

"What could I possibly be mad about? The fact that because of you, I'm trapped in a barn with two deranged rednecks wanting to have fun with me? No, of course not," said Tracy.

"Tracy, it's not like I meant for this to happen," said Leon.

"Well, you should have been more careful! Instead of breaking the speed limit and getting us run off the road by a rogue cop," said Tracy.

"We were on the back roads; there wasn't supposed to be anyone out there!" said Leon.

"Look, Leon, if I hadn't gotten in that car with you, I could have been at Jim's right now. We could have been watching Private Eyes, a series I actually think is very inventive and funny. We could have talked about his cases or what life in DC was like. But instead, I chose to trust you, and look where it got me," said Tracy.

"Tracy, what about our moment, the kissing? Didn't you enjoy that?" asked Leon.

"Yeah, I only wish I had some mouthwash with me. Just leave me alone, Leon!" said Tracy.

"Now look here. You heard her." Leon tried to get forceful with Tracy, but Jimmy came over.

"She said to leave her alone," said Jimmy.

"Or else what?" said Leon.

"Do you really want these three women to see you get your ass kicked while trapped in a smelly old barn?" asked Jimmy as Leon started to back down.

"I think I'll just go and sit down over there," said Leon as he walked away.

"Thanks, Jimmy," said Tracy.

"Anytime," said Jimmy.

"You okay? And I don't mean about the current situation," said Tracy.

Jimmy was trying to stop himself from crying.

"He wasn't a bad guy, Tracy….Derek may have done some wrong things, but he wasn't a bad guy," said Jimmy.

"Jimmy, I'm sorry," said Tracy.

"It's my fault he died, you know," said Jimmy.

"Why is it your fault?" asked Tracy.

"I'm the one that got him into underage drinking. His dad told him to stay away from me, said I was bad news…..and yet he defied him because apparently, I was the most fun guy he'd ever met," said Jimmy.

"I made him like that, and…..it's what got him killed!" said Jimmy as he finally broke down in tears.

"Oh, Jimmy, come here," said Tracy as she hugged him.

"It's not your fault; none of it is your fault," said Tracy as she stopped hugging him.

"Well, they won't get away with it that much, I promise," said Jimmy.

"I don't know what's going to happen to us. But that cop who shot Derek, one way or another, I'm going to kill him," said Jimmy.

"Jimmy, you have to know the odds are against you," said Tracy.

"I don't care. Even if I die trying, I owe Derek that much," said Jimmy.

"Jimmy, what exactly is your plan? Ambush one of the rednecks and take their gun?" asked Tracy.

"Maybe, perhaps, when they come back, the two of us can jump them," said Jimmy.

"You may be willing to suicide by redneck, but I'm not. We have to wait, bide our time," said Tracy.

"For what? For Jim to ride in on horseback and save the day?" said Jimmy.

"He will come; he's probably out there right now, looking for me and the rest of us," said Tracy.

"In the meantime, we can't let these guys get to us. We stay strong and don't let them turn us into farm animals," said Tracy as she looked through the crack and saw Cletus approaching.

"One of them is coming," said Tracy as she stepped back; Jimmy took cover at the side.

"What are you doing?!" asked Tracy.

"Ambush, they'll never see it coming," said Jimmy.

"Can you step away from the door, please?" said Cletus from outside.

"Shit," said Jimmy as he backed away.

Cletus opened the door and came in, holding his shotgun in one hand and a plate of what looked like sliced bread in the other. He carefully placed it on the ground inside the barn.

"Eat up, everyone. There's a slice for each of you, so don't get greedy. Can't have you all starving to death, not when there's more fun to be had," said Cletus as he left the barn and locked the door.

Everyone looked at the plate of dried bread. Soon, they all dived for it; they each took a slice and started eating rather quickly.

Tracy stopped and looked at Jimmy, who looked back at her.

"What was that about not turning us into farm animals?" said Jimmy.

Tracy just sighed and went back to eating.

Chapter 10
Initiative and Deceit

Shaw's Bar, Evening 10:30 pm

Jim walked down the street to Shaw's Bar, ready to attend the secret meeting the Sheriff had set up.

He knocked on the door after seeing the blinds were down on the windows, and the closed sign was up.

"Who is it?" asked Shaw from inside.

"It's Jim Gold," said Jim.

"What's the password?" asked Shaw.

"I don't have a password," said Jim as the door unlocked and opened.

"Come on in," said Shaw as he let Jim inside, then closed and locked the door again.

Jim saw the Sheriff sitting at a big table with Joey, Min, Dom, Violet and Eileen.

"Come on over, Jim, have a seat," said Sheriff Hanson as Jim sat down.

"Quite a place for a secret meeting," said Jim.

"In case of emergency, this is neutral ground for us. Also, we get free drinks in a crisis," said Sheriff Hanson as everyone laughed.

"No disrespect, Shaw," said Sheriff Hanson.

"None taken, Sheriff," said Shaw with a smile on his face.

"Now then, I call this meeting to order. As we already know, five teenage cars have all disappeared off the back roads of Pike County in the last month. Things were already tense before Derek Johnson and his friends disappeared…..but now young Tracy Kean has become the same," said Sheriff Hanson.

"And our fair town has since been invaded by the FBI. Agent Francis Morgan has asked us to be "cooperative" and "helpful" during his little investigation to find some spoiled rich brat, no indication of helping us find our missing people," said Sheriff Hanson.

"So what do we do, Sheriff?" asked Joey.

"Well, we have one thing they don't: we know this town from top to bottom; we've protected and looked after it way longer than they were in the academy. We know the people, we know the buildings, we know who to talk to, we know where to hide, we know every hidden tunnel and secret door there is around here," said Sheriff Hanson.

"Sheriff, we don't have any secret tunnels or hidden doors," said Joey.

"I was talking metaphorically, Joey," said Sheriff Hanson.

"So what's the next step?" asked Jim.

"Well, the next thing I'm going to suggest won't feel like a popular choice, but it's all we've got. We need to work with the

FBI," said Sheriff Hanson as everyone started speaking all at once.

"Calm down, calm down, let me finish," said Sheriff Hanson.

"These guys like to think they're of a higher standard just cause they're from the big city. Now, I'm not saying we have to make friends with them…I'm suggesting we use them," said Sheriff Hanson.

"You see, as much as we may not agree with them when something like this happens, we investigate as much as possible, and then we hand it over to the county police. But the FBI has the resources that'll cut our search patterns in half," said Sheriff Hanson.

"So, we use a little trickery and deception to get them to help us find the missing teens. By the time they realise what's happened, we will have both accomplished our goals," said Sheriff Hanson.

"Creating false leads to manipulate the FBI into helping us? I have to admit, Sheriff, it sounds a bit risky," said Jim.

"I know, and we're all aware of getting dog collars put around our necks. But, like it or not, we can't find Tracy and the others without their help. I mean, with time, we probably could, but we don't have that much time," said Sheriff Hanson.

"For now, we focus on any other leads we may have. Anything that may give us an edge before the FBI interferes," said Sheriff Hanson.

"You know, I still haven't had the chance to talk to Mr Johnson about Derek. Maybe I could ask him a few of my own questions," said Jim.

"If you think it'll help, then go ahead," said Sheriff Hanson.

"Hey, when we were talking about the county police, I actually had an old school friend who worked for them. I mean, we haven't spoken for a while, but if I can get him to come here, maybe he has some theories about what could have happened on the roads," said Joey.

"That's something too. See, we're getting there," said Sheriff Hanson.

"What about the rest of us?" asked Min.

"Well, Min, I'm afraid you and Dom will be questioning the parents of Cassie, Tammy and Jimmy, the most recent to go missing. Find out what they know and if there's a reason something like this would happen," said Sheriff Hanson.

"What about me and Eileen, Uncle Reg?" asked Violet.

"Well, Violet, you and Eileen have the most important job. You have to keep the town calm and stop everyone from rioting with pitchforks and torches. We don't need the FBI cracking down any more than they are already," said Sheriff Hanson.

"No pressure then," said Violet.

"What will you be doing, Sheriff?" asked Jim.

"I sadly have the job of keeping a close eye on Agent Morgan and making sure he doesn't do anything untoward or illegal during his investigation", said Sheriff Hanson.

"Look at this; we have a whole team and the spirit that we can do this," said Jim.

"Go, team!" said Eileen as she held out her hand across the table. Everyone looked for a moment, and she then felt embarrassed.

"Go, team," said Jim as he placed his hand on Eileen's.

"Go team", said Violet as she did the same; the others quickly joined in doing the same.

"Go, team," said Sheriff Hanson as he was the last one to do it.

Jim was right; they were a team, and they had the spirit. They could do it.

Johnson Residence, the next morning 9:30 am

Violet's morning broadcast sounded over the radios in town.

"Good morning, Milford; it's another lovely day outside with a small chance of rain later this evening, so it's the perfect time to get out there and soak up that sun. Now, rumours have been spreading that the FBI are in town, and I'm here to tell you folks that it's all true. Agent Francis Morgan has asked that everyone please be cooperative during his investigation. All I'll say, folks is try your best to answer their questions and don't let them get under your skin. Sheriff Hanson and Jim Gold are still on the case, and we all wish them the best of luck. In the meantime, let's all keep praying for the safe return of Tracy, Derek and the other missing teens," said Violet over the radio.

Jim walked over to the Johnson residence in the centre of town, another bungalow-type building, but much wider in width. He walked up the stone porch to the front door and knocked. No sooner had Jim done it, he was greeted by a man in his sixties with a walking stick; this was Mr Johnson, Derek's father. The stick was for a condition that made him a bit weak in the legs.

"Jim, thank you for coming round," said Mr Johnson.

"Thank you for agreeing to see me, Mr Johnson," said Jim as he was invited inside.

The living space was about the same as you'd expect in a normal household.

"I just made some coffee. Would you like a cup?" said Mr Johnson.

"That'd be great, thanks" said Jim.

"Take a seat in the living room, and I'll be with you", said Mr Johnson as he pointed to the living room, then walked off to the kitchen. Jim sat down on the couch and waited for him to come back.

Mr Johnson came in with a single cup of coffee and handed it to Jim.

"Thanks, you're not having one?" said Jim.

"Had it before you came, trying to psych myself up for the interview?" said Mr Johnson as he sat down opposite Jim.

"You know, when Derek didn't come home that night, I did consider hiring you to find him. Of course, I know you're bound by the same jurisdiction rule as the Sheriff," said Mr Johnson.

"Despite that, I'd still like to try and help Mr Johnson. I know I can only go so far, but maybe it'll be enough," said Jim.

"So, what would you like to know?" asked Mr Johnson.

"I only know so much about Derek, but I have heard some things suggesting he was a man about the town," said Jim.

"Well, when you live in a town like this, you can only go so far. Every parent wants to be proud of his children, and for the most part, Derek has a good future ahead of him. But then his mother died, and he met Jimmy Pascal," said Mr Johnson.

"You blame Jimmy for Derek's change of character?" asked Jim.

"You're damn right I do, ever since they met, Derek was out at all hours. I got told that he'd been throwing eggs at people's windows, and the cheeky devils even started going for joyrides in my car. You have no idea how many repairs I've paid for," said Mr Johnson.

"You didn't get Derek to pay for the repairs?" asked Jim.

"No, I wanted to. But the only money he has is what he's been saving up for college, and his mother would've haunted me for making him fork it over just to fix a dent in the bumper," said Mr Johnson.

"I was desperate to ground him forever when he started drinking and ditching class," said Mr Johnson.

"And that was all Jimmy's doing, too?" asked Jim.

"You bet it was, skipping class and underage drinking, his mother was probably turning in her grave. I finally had it out with him before the start of this year, and I told him that he had to change his ways or else his whole life would spiral out of control," said Mr Johnson.

"And did he listen?" asked Jim.

"For the most part, he did. In the last six months, he showed real improvement. I even gave him my car for his eighteenth birthday to show him how proud I was of him," said Mr Johnson.

"And then he takes off with it, and now he's disappeared," said Mr Johnson.

"Can you think of any reason why this might happen? Asked Jim.

"I'm sure some people think he's just run away. But we were getting along again; we were talking and doing stuff together. I….I can't believe that he'd do this to me," said Mr Johnson.

"You know I promised my wife I'd look after him, that I'd educate him and bring him upright. Yeah, a fat lot of good I've done," said Mr Johnson.

"You are a good dad, Mr Johnson; this is probably just a misunderstanding. Maybe Derek took the car to the next town over. He's broken down, and he's trying to get it repaired," said Jim.

"I appreciate what you're saying, Jim. Maybe you're right, this might just be…wait a minute…the next town…the next town," said Mr Johnson as he suddenly got up from his armchair.

"What is it?" asked Jim as he got up too.

"Come with me," said Mr Johnson as he led Jim through the kitchen and to his bedroom at the back of the house. He started rummaging around on his nightstand. Jim just stood there and waited for him to finish.

Mr Johnson finally emerged with a small device.

"Yes, I knew I still had it," said Mr Johnson.

"What is that?" asked Jim.

"It's a remote for the tracker I put in Derek's phone," said Mr Johnson.

"You put a tracker in his phone?" asked Jim.

"It was actually a while ago, which is why I didn't think of it. Four years ago, Derek went on a school trip to the city. On the way back, he was so exhausted that he got on the wrong bus and ended up in the wrong town. He called me, and I spent ages trying to find him because he didn't know where he was," said Mr Johnson.

"His mother had the idea of putting the tracker in his phone, and I agreed with it. We didn't tell him, though," said Mr Johnson.

"Understandable. So why is the remote on the nightstand with dust on it?" asked Jim.

"Well, after that day, Derek never got on the wrong bus during a trip again, so I just filed this away and forgot about it. But I don't believe that Derek has changed his phone, so the tracker should still be active," said Mr Johnson as he tried to turn on the remote, but nothing happened.

"Damn it, it's stopped working," said Mr Johnson.

"Well, let me take it to the station. I'm sure one of our more technically minded people can get it working again," said Jim.

"This is the first solid lead we've gotten, Mr Johnson, thank you," said Jim.

"Thanks, Jim. I really hope it helps, and I really hope that Derek isn't in too much trouble," said Mr Johnson.

"Thanks for the coffee, Mr Johnson; I'll let you know if we find anything," said Jim as he headed out.

"Jim, I heard about Tracy. I really hope you find her too," said Mr Johnson.

"So do I," said Jim as he left the house.

Shortly after he did, his mobile rang, the caller ID showed Joey's name.

"Hey, Joey," said Jim.

"Hey Jim, how did it go with Mr Johnson?" asked Joey.

"Pretty good, actually; he gave me a remote that connects to a tracker he put in Derek's phone a while ago. It's not working at the moment, but I'm thinking that Francis should be able to reactivate it," said Jim.

"How are you going to convince Francis to reactivate it?" asked Joey.

"I think I'm going to have to tell him that it's a universal remote, capable of picking up any phone trackers within a few miles," said Jim.

"So, lie to him," said Joey.

"Manipulating is more the word," said Jim.

"Uh, I'm still not keen on the Sheriff's idea of working with the FBI," said Joey.

"We're not working with them, we're using them," said Jim.

"Okay, well, I don't like the whole lie and deceive them part. They're still powerful people, and I'm actually a little worried about the whole dog collar thing," said Joey.

"We'll be fine, Joey. Remember that I was once one of them. I know how they work, and I know how to trick them," said Jim.

"Yeah, great. Anyway, when you've dropped that remote off, can you come to the diner? My high school friend in the County police has agreed to meet us there," said Joey.

"That's great, Joey; I'll be there soon," said Jim as he put the phone down and headed back for the station.

Milford Diner, Morning 10:00 am

After dropping the remote off and surprisingly fooling Francis into believing it was universal, Jim headed for the diner. The diner was owned by a young woman named Rose. She was a very sweet 25-year-old girl who loved pretty much everyone, and the diner was a nice, well-kept place for meals and meetings.

Jim entered the diner and was immediately greeted by Rose.

"Hey Jim," said Rose.

"Hey Rose, how's business?" asked Jim.

"Business is good, thanks for asking. Hey, I heard about Tracy, is there any news?" said Rose.

"Not yet, we're looking at every possible angle for information," said Jim.

"Oh, I really wish I could tell you something that would help," said Rose.

"You know what would help? Some of your famous blueberry pie," said Jim.

"But I thought you only had that at lunchtime," said Rose.

"Consider this a cheat day," said Jim as Rose giggled and went to get the pie.

Joey suddenly walked in with another young man dressed in a cop uniform, both talking and then laughing at something funny.

"Hey Jim, this is my friend I was telling you about," said Joey.

"Jim Gold," said Jim as he extended his hand.

"Boles, Frank Boles" said Frank.

Rose came back with Jim's pie slice.

"Here's your pie, Jim….oh…who's your friend?" said Rose, looking at Frank.

"Frank Boles, County police, here for your protection, madam," said Frank.

"What do I need protection from?" asked Rose.

"I don't know, something," said Frank with a laugh; Rose giggled.

"Would you like a slice of blueberry pie, too?" asked Rose.

"I'd love one," said Frank as Rose walked away with a big smile.

"I'd like one too, Rose. Still the ladies' man, huh?" said Joey.

"They can't resist me," said Frank.

"Why don't we go sit down?" said Jim as he took his pie, and the three of them sat down at one of the tables. Rose quickly brought over two more pie slices for Frank and Joey.

"Thanks, cutie," said Frank as Rose smiled and walked away again.

"So, you know Joey from high school?" asked Jim.

"Yep, we spent a good number of years together and got into a few fights as well", said Frank.

"You guys fought each other?" asked Jim.

"No, he means fighting with other people. We tried to become law-keepers for the school, defending the other kids from being beaten up by the bullies," said Joey.

"Yeah, and then we were the ones that got beat up," said Frank as he and Joey laughed.

"So, has Joey filled you in on what's been happening?" asked Jim.

"He has, although I've already been hearing about it through work. It's been getting passed around like a ghost story, all those teenagers," said Frank.

"Do you have any idea if someone might be behind the disappearances?" asked Jim.

"Well, Mr Gold, we get all sorts of crazies living out there. Rednecks, hillbillies, cannibals and even serial killers hiding from the law," said Frank.

"Are any of them active in the area?" asked Jim.

"To be honest, I wouldn't be surprised if they were all active in the area. I mean, we catch as many as we can, but there are some out there who can evade us for months, even years. One guy I remember stayed out there for ten years before he was captured," said Frank.

"Did any of them specialise in kidnapping teenagers?" asked Jim.

"Well, they took just about anyone. But specifically teenagers? That's a new one," said Frank.

"Is there any way you can help us?" asked Jim.

"Well, I can check the archives back at my station to see if there's anyone specific in the area of Milford. And maybe a reason why they're targeting teens," said Frank.

"That would be a big help, buddy," said Joey.

"Always happy to help. Now come on, this pie isn't going to eat itself," said Frank as the three of them started tucking into their pie slices.

The rest of the conversation went ahead, with Joey and Frank reminiscing about old times and Jim getting in the occasional question about who might be behind the kidnappings. Finally, Frank said he had to leave, but he'd be in touch with any new information. Jim went with Joey back to the Sheriff's department to find out the progress on the tracker.

Chapter 11
A Dark Discovery

Milford Sheriff's Department: Morning 10:30 am

Jim entered the station with Joey and walked over to the office area where Francis had set up his investigation. The room was mostly filled with a table of scattered documents, two laptops and a large whiteboard with a few pictures attached to it.

"Ah, Jim, I was just about to call you. We've had a development," said Francis.

"You got the remote working?" asked Jim.

"When you've worked in the FBI for as long as I have, you learn a trick or two on how to reactivate old technology," said Francis.

"I just replaced some of the wirings, gave it a new battery and now (he shows the remote with a red dot on the screen, making a slow single beep noise again and again), we have a signal," said Francis.

"It appears to lead out of town. With luck, this might be Leon's phone," said Francis.

"Yeah," said Jim as Joey gave an uneasy smile.

"Okay, get the Sheriff and round up some deputies. We're going to follow this signal to the source; let's move out," said

Francis as he and other agents left the room. Jim followed with an unsure-looking Joey.

The Back Roads of Pike County, Morning 11:00 am

After gathering together and discussing the plan, three cars left Milford and began following the signal along the back roads. Francis was in front while the Sheriff was driving behind with Jim, Joey and Min in the police car. Another car with a few deputies was following at the back.

"I don't like this," said Joey.

"I don't either, but we have to find out what happened to Derek and the others. Just pray it's not the worst-case scenario," said Sheriff Hanson.

"I didn't mean that. I mean, I did a bit, but I meant I don't like all this lying to Francis," said Joey.

"When he finds out that the signal is leading us to Derek and not Leon, he isn't going to be happy," said Joey.

"You let us worry about Francis, Joey. This is the first proper lead we've gotten, and it may be the start of getting some answers," said Jim.

"Yeah, otherwise, it's dog collars," said Joey.

"He's not going to collar us, Joey. We've only lied to him once; we still have two more strikes to go," said Sheriff Hanson.

"Oh great, we're comparing baseball now," said Joey.

Sheriff Hanson checked his car's GPS.

"We're quite a ways from town; they must have been going some speed to achieve this distance," said Sheriff Hanson.

"Because they were joyriding or running away from something?" asked Jim.

The car in front of them started to slow down.

"Francis is slowing down," said Min as the convoy came to a stop.

Francis and the agents got out, Sheriff Hanson and the others did the same. Francis was pacing up and down with the remote in his hand.

"We're very close, Sheriff; the signal is somewhere around here," said Francis as he walked towards the embankment on the left side.

"The signal is coming from down there," said Francis as everyone went to take a look.

They could see the remains of a car that had rolled a few metres away from the embankment.

"Joey, Min, get the ropes," said Sheriff Hanson as Joey and Min carried out the task.

They collected long lengths of rope with hooks from their car, attached the hooks to the back of the car and threw the ropes down the embankment. Everyone started climbing down individually; Joey helped Min with the last few inches as she came down.

"Thanks", said Min.

"Anytime," said Joey.

The deputies from the other car remained at the top to keep an eye on the ropes and for anyone coming down the road.

The group below carefully approached the car wreck.

"Be careful; sometimes wild folk like to claim car wrecks as their residence, and they're very timid", said Sheriff Hanson as they reached the car and looked inside.

It wasn't that bad, aside from the damage on the outside. Sheriff Hanson checked the licence plate.

"Well?" asked Jim.

"It's Mr Johnson's car, alright," said Sheriff Hanson.

"Whose?" asked Francis.

Nobody responded as he checked the signal again.

"According to the remote, the signal is right here, but I don't see anything," said Francis.

"Maybe we just need to spread out a bit, check every WHOA!" Joey suddenly fell to the floor mid-sentence.

"Joey, you okay?" asked Min as she ran over to him.

"Yeah, I'm okay, I'm okay, just tripped on something, probably a rock or-ARGH!!!" Joey suddenly screamed as he saw what he'd tripped on.

Everyone came running over and expressed shocked looks as they saw it, too. A body partly buried by leaves and only just starting to decay.

"Sheriff, is that….." Jim couldn't finish his sentence.

"Yes, Jim. It's Derek Johnson," said Sheriff Hanson.

The Back Roads of Pike County, Morning 11:35 am

The next half hour was filled with waiting for backup from the County police to help excavate the vehicle and get Derek's body to the ambulance for transportation back to Milford. It would have made sense to send them both to another facility for evidence gathering and an autopsy. But despite being lied to, Agent Morgan wanted to know for certain if there was something that would connect to Leon Thornberg's disappearance.

"I still can't believe you both lied to me," said Francis.

"We didn't exactly lie; we...embellished the truth a bit," said Sheriff Hanson.

"Embellish my ass; you wasted valuable FBI time during a vital investigation," said Francis.

"Vital" Jim scoffed.

"Excuse me?" said Francis.

"You're out here searching for some rich kid to return home to mommy and daddy. While we actually have kids with parents who care about them going missing up here, and you don't seem to give a damn!" said Jim.

"I have my job to do, and I thought I made it clear that we have to work together while I'm here," said Francis.

"We are working together, but there's one thing you need to understand. Derek was a local, a part of the town, so we're a little anxious to find out exactly what happened to him. Now there's every chance that there may be something which leads to figuring out what became of Leon, and if that's the case, we will have both achieved something," said Sheriff Hanson.

"Well, that's why I'm having the body and the car taken back to town. If there is something, then we need to find it quickly and remember, I was serious about those dog collars," said Francis as he walked away.

"Jackass," said Sheriff Hanson.

"You said it," said Jim as they both stood there quietly for a bit.

"Sheriff…." said Jim.

"I know Jim. But from the looks of it, Derek's been dead for a while, more than likely before we realised he was missing. So no….there was nothing either you or I could've done," said Sheriff Hanson.

"Doesn't make it any better, though?" said Jim.

"It's got me thinking about Tracy, too. These aren't just simple disappearances anymore, Sheriff; they've most likely become kidnappings and now murder," said Jim.

"We've got to keep positive, though, Jim. We couldn't help Derek, but if he can help get us some answers, maybe we can save the others," said Sheriff Hanson.

"I hope you're right," said Jim.

"Look, Jim, there's also one other thing we need to deal with, and if you'd rather, I can get someone else," said Sheriff Hanson.

"No, Sheriff, it should be me. I'll tell Mr Johnson," said Jim.

Johnson Residence, Afternoon 12:05 pm

Jim returned to the town with everyone else and walked the rest of the way to the Johnson house. His heart was in his mouth, and he felt sick. He'd made a promise to find Derek, and now he was about to inform Mr Johnson that he'd broken that promise, even though he hadn't intended to.

Jim walked up to the door and knocked. Mr Johnson answered pretty quickly.

"Jim, I didn't expect to see you back so soon," said Mr Johnson. Jim was quiet.

"What's wrong?" asked Mr Johnson.

"I'm really, really sorry, Mr Johnson," said Jim.

"What…no….no, no, no, don't….don't you say it!" said Mr Johnson.

"We found Derek….I'm afraid he's dead," said Jim as Mr Johnson suddenly fell to the floor as the shock made his legs give out.

"Mr Johnson!" said Jim as he ran over to him.

Mr Johnson broke down in tears; Jim felt like doing the same; he really hated **breaking a promise.**

Chapter 12
The Search for Clues

Milford Clinic, Afternoon 12:10 pm

The Milford Clinic was where Doctor Mcallister worked, along with a few nurses and medical volunteers. They were quite well stocked with medical supplies and capable of performing basic operations and procedures. But anything more than that required them to give it to a city hospital.

In the morgue section at the back, Doctor Mcallister, Francis, Sheriff Hanson and Min were staring down at Derek's body on the slab. Joey had been sent to deal with handling the delivery of the car wreck to the station.

"Now, this body could hold something important for us. So you need to get anything you can from it," said Francis as Doctor Mcallister looked at him.

"This body has a name, Derek Johnson. I watched this kid grow up from a toddler; show some respect," said Doctor Mcallister.

"I apologise, but I need to know if you're capable of doing this autopsy," said Francis.

"Listen, Sonny, I used to be a city coroner. I was performing autopsies back when you were still writing on the walls and running around in a diaper," said Doctor Mcallister as Min and Sheriff Hanson laughed quietly.

"Now granted, when I got my doctor's licence and moved down here, I thought I'd seen the last of looking at a body on the slab. But from time to time, I have to deal with youngsters who drowned while swimming in the lakes or hunters who let their prey get the better of them," said Doctor Mcallister.

"So you can do it?" asked Francis.

"Yes, I can do it," said Doctor Mcallister.

"Good, don't let personal feelings get in the way; the guy's dead now, can't do anything about it. Now then, Sheriff, let's see if any progress has been made on the car," said Francis as he walked out of the room.

"When can I expect his body on the slab?" asked Doctor Mcallister.

"Getting sooner all the time, Doc," said Sheriff Hanson as he and Min left, too.

Milford Sheriff's Department, Afternoon 12:20 pm

In the impound section at the back of the station, Joey was supervising the evidence collection from the car. Sheriff Hanson, Min and Francis walked over to the wreck.

"How's it going, Joey?" asked Sheriff Hanson.

"Still looking it over. But there are a few things of interest we've found over here," said Joey as he led them to a small table with a few items on it.

"Now we're still collecting fingerprints; most likely, they belong to either Derek or the others in the car. But we also found these two whiskey bottles, the good stuff; I recognised them from Shaw's Bar," said Joey.

"They pilfered whiskey from Shaw's?" asked Min.

"Seems they did," said Joey.

"These bottles are empty; were they drunk?" asked Sheriff Hanson.

"Well, it's likely, Sheriff. We've found a few spill stains on the seats, so, yeah, they were most likely drinking," said Joey.

"Okay, pull everything together and send it to the lab," said Sheriff Hanson.

"Can I just ask, how long does it take for something to get back from the lab?" asked Francis.

"Um, well, on a bad day, a week. But on a good day, about…..five days," said Sheriff Hanson.

"Five days?!" said Francis.

"Give or take a day," said Min.

"I'm not waiting that long for something that could be vital to my investigation. Give me the number of the lab, and let me talk to them," said Francis.

"Are you sure about that?" asked Sheriff Hanson.

"I'm sure; let me have the number," said Francis.

"Alright, talk to Kelly at the front desk; she has the number. Tell her I sent you," said Sheriff Hanson.

"Thank you," said Francis as he walked away.

"So, did you find anything else, Joey?" asked Sheriff Hanson.

"A set of fingerprints on the driver's side door and what looks like a boot print on the back of the car, like he was kicking it, or maybe pushing it," said Joey.

"The car went down an embankment; it certainly wasn't a crash. Otherwise, we would have found the other teens, too," said Sheriff Hanson.

"And Derek, that gunshot wound to his head, he didn't die in the car," said Min.

"I've seen that kind of wound before. It was no accident; it was an execution," said Sheriff Hanson.

"Someone executed Derek? What the hell is going on, Sheriff?!" asked Joey.

"I wish I knew Joey, I wish I knew," said Sheriff Hanson.

Milford Sheriff's Department, Afternoon 12:30 pm

Sheriff Hanson gathered Joey, Min and Dom together in the station to talk about theories following Derek's possible execution. Jim walked in a while later with Mr Johnson next to him.

"Sheriff," said Jim.

"Jim, Mr Johnson, I'm very sorry. Derek was a good kid," said Sheriff Hanson.

"He was, Sheriff, he was. Jim took me to see his body, and we caught Doctor Mcallister as he was finishing his autopsy. I just wanted to see my boy's face," said Mr Johnson.

"Mr Johnson, it's obviously been a shock to you. Why don't you go home and rest?" said Jim.

"Yeah, rest, like I'll be able to do that again," said Mr Johnson.

"I'll get someone to take you home. Dom, can you do it?" said Sheriff Hanson.

"Sure thing, Sheriff," said Dom as he started walking Mr Johnson outside. But he stopped when he noticed Francis walking towards them.

"Is that him, the FBI guy?" asked Mr Johnson.

"Yeah, that's him," said Dom as Mr Johnson suddenly started approaching him. Jim and the others followed.

"Excuse me, are you the FBI guy who just arrived in town?" asked Mr Johnson.

"Yeah, Special Agent Francis Morgan, and you are?" said Francis.

"I'm Alex Johnson. Derek Johnson was my son," said Mr Johnson.

"Oh, I see. Well, I'm sorry, Mr Johnson, it was a nasty way to go," said Francis.

"Oh, screw your apologies; when are you going to get off your ass and do something about it?!" said Mr Johnson.

"Well, Mr Johnson, we're very busy with our own investigation at the moment. We're still looking into every possible lead," said Francis.

"Oh, piss on your leads; you know damn well who's behind this! Because the FBI always likes to know everything and keep the public in the dark about it. You know who killed my son, don't you?!" said Mr Johnson, getting angry.

"Mr Johnson, you're mistaken. Now, I know you're most likely going through a lot of emotions that are messing with your head, and you're saddened by the fact that your son was drinking prior to his death, but we don't know anything else. In fact, it's likely that he pissed off some other car driver who decided to pop him and chuck him off the road. Sucks to be him for sure," said Francis as Mr Johnson suddenly lifted his cane and tried to swing for Francis, but Jim and the others stopped him and held onto him so he didn't fall.

"He's lucky that didn't get me because I would have arrested him for assaulting a federal agent!" said Francis.

"He just lost his son, Francis; give him a break!" said Jim.

"Okay, calm down, everyone. Dom, please take Mr Johnson home, and Agent Morgan, please shut your mouth!" said Sheriff Hanson as Dom escorted Mr Johnson out of the station.

Everyone tried to calm down.

Shortly after, Doctor Mcallister came in.

"Is everything okay?" asked Doctor Mcallister.

"We're fine, Doc," said Min.

"Well, good, 'cause I have the finished autopsy here," said Doctor Mcallister.

"Perfect, let's take it into the office," said Francis.

"Oh, Sheriff and Jim Gold only, no deputies," said Francis as he headed for the office. Sheriff Hanson and Jim followed while Joey and Min stayed in the main area.

Temporary FBI Office, Afternoon 12:49

In the FBI office area, Doctor Mcallister showed the pictures he'd taken and the results of the various blood tests he'd done.

"As much as I hate to admit it, there are clear signs that Derek was intoxicated while in the car. He'd only had a slurp, though, from what I can tell," said Doctor Mcallister.

"Cause of death was, as I'm sure many of you already suspected, a gunshot wound to the head, but there's more. I found another gunshot that entered his back. I extracted bullets from both wounds, and I'll be sending them to the lab," said Doctor Mcallister.

"Do you have any idea which wound came first?" asked Jim.

"Actually, yes, my examination shows that the back wound was first. Now, the wound suggests a pistol round, but it was fired from a small distance. Then the wound to the head was at close range, and that finished him," said Doctor Mcallister.

"So, maybe Derek was trying to run away from someone, whoever took his friends?" asked Jim.

"Yeah, but here's another thing: it wasn't a fair fight. I found these bruising marks around his wrists. Now, the only time I've seen this is when people have tried to sue the Sheriff for putting on the cuffs too tight," said Doctor Mcallister.

"So, you're saying Derek was handcuffed before he was shot?" asked Sheriff Hanson.

"It looks like it," said Doctor Mcallister.

"Sheriff, could we be dealing with a cop?" asked Jim. Sheriff Hanson didn't respond.

"If it is a cop, we need those results back as soon as possible," said Francis.

"How did your call with them go?" asked Sheriff Hanson.

"They said they'll put it in the fast track lane, but you know how it is, lots to do, things to examine. If we were in Washington, it wouldn't be a problem," said Francis.

Jim was about to say something when someone started hammering at the door. He went over and opened it; Min came in with a worried look on her face.

"Sheriff, we've got a problem!" said Min.

"What is it?" asked Sheriff Hanson.

"We had a call saying that a gunshot was heard from the Johnson residence. Joey went to investigate, but he said Mr Johnson came out brandishing a handgun and threatened him to stay away," said Min.

"What the hell is Alex playing at? We better get down there," said Sheriff Hanson.

"Wait, Sheriff, there's more. Mr Johnson told Joey he has a hostage, and if anyone tries to enter the house, he'll kill him," said Min.

"Do we know who the hostage is?" asked Jim.

"I wasn't sure at first, then it dawned on me. Dom hasn't come back since escorting Mr Johnson home, and he's not answering his radio," said Min.

"Oh Christ," said Sheriff Hanson.

Chapter 13
Hostage Negotiations

Johnson Residence, Afternoon 12:55 pm

The sound of approaching police cars soon arrived outside the Johnson residence. Joey was already there just outside the porch area. The cars all screeched to a halt, and deputies armed with pistols and shotguns took their positions and aimed at the house. Sheriff Hanson, Jim and Min approached Joey, taking cover behind his car as they did. Francis was, unfortunately, with them too.

"What's happening, Joey?" asked Sheriff Hanson.

"I don't know, Sheriff. Ever since Mr Johnson told me he had a hostage and told me to stay away, he's been really quiet," said Joey.

"Have you been able to reach Dom?" asked Jim.

"I've been trying, but he's not picking up. Either his radio's off or…..actually, you don't want me to finish that," said Joey.

"Sheriff, the megaphone is ready for you," said one of the deputies as he handed the receiver to the Sheriff.

"Alex Johnson, this is Sheriff Reginald Hanson. We understand you may be holding one of my deputies hostage. Now, I'd rather that this doesn't end with violence. Just let Dom go and surrender peacefully, then maybe we can talk about this," said Sheriff Hanson into the megaphone.

There was no response.

"Come on, Alex, don't make this harder than it already is. This isn't you, just think about what you're doing," said Sheriff Hanson.

There was still no response.

"This isn't working. Sheriff, you need to go in there and contain the situation," said Francis.

"When I want your opinion, I'll ask for it. This is my town, and one of my deputies is in there!" said Sheriff Hanson.

"Sheriff, let me have a try," said Jim.

"Go ahead," said Sheriff Hanson as he handed the receiver to Jim.

"Mr Johnson, this is Jim Gold. Now I know that you're hurting right now, and I don't want anyone else to get hurt. So I'd like to make a deal with you; I'm going to approach the house," said Jim as everyone looked surprised.

"I'm going to come inside so that we can talk about this and hopefully resolve the situation peacefully; I will be alone and unarmed. Once I put this receiver down, I'm going to walk up to the house with my hands in the air. If you want me to come in, open the front door a crack, and I'll be there in a minute," said Jim as he put the receiver down and started walking around the cop car.

"Wait a minute, you can't do this!" said Francis as Jim just stared at him and kept on walking.

"You can't let him do this, Sheriff; he's not law enforcement!" said Francis.

"Just let him do his job," said Sheriff Hanson.

"I didn't realise Hostage Negotiation was in a private investigator's resume," said Francis.

"Excuse me, Agent Morgan?" said Joey.

"What?" asked Francis.

"Could you shut up, please?" said Joey as Sheriff Hanson and Min smiled; Francis didn't say anything.

Jim slowly walked down the stone porch with his hands slightly raised in the air; his heart was beating pretty fast. It'd been a long time since he'd talked down an armed man with a hostage, but he had to try, for Mr Johnson's safety as well as Dom's. As he got closer to the house, the front door opened a crack; Jim pushed the door and went inside, closing it as he did.

Everything was quiet inside.

"Mr Johnson?" said Jim.

"In here," said Mr Johnson's voice from the living room.

Jim entered and found Mr Johnson sitting in his armchair with a handgun. He also noticed Dom on the sofa; he was holding a cloth to his shoulder, it was partially bloodied.

"Take a seat," said Mr Johnson as Jim sat down next to Dom.

"How are you, Mr Johnson?" asked Jim.

"I've been better, Jim. This is the first time I've pulled out this gun and taken a hostage," said Mr Johnson.

"You okay, Dom?" asked Jim.

"Yeah, I'm fine; it's just a flesh wound. I'll live," said Dom.

"I didn't mean to do that, but I had to stop him from leaving," said Mr Johnson.

"Mr Johnson, why do this? What do you hope to gain?" asked Jim.

"What I hope to gain, Jim, is some damn attention from those FBI scum. They know way more about the disappearances than they're letting on; they're just too stubborn and prideful to admit it!" said Mr Johnson.

"So why the hostage?" asked Jim.

"Because I've already been spreading rumours about the FBI's presence since they arrived, explaining my concerns to my friends and neighbours. If I kill Dom and myself, then the town will rise up against those agents and demand they bring in more people and resources to find out what the hell is happening on those back roads!" said Mr Johnson.

"Mr Johnson, hasn't enough blood already been spilt? Do you really think that more will solve anything?" asked Jim.

"You saw Derek's body, Jim, the bullet wound to his head. He may have done some bad things, but he was a good boy, and he didn't deserve to be executed like an animal!" said Mr Johnson.

"How do you know that it was an execution?" asked Jim as Mr Johnson looked over at Dom.

"Sorry, I wasn't thinking," said Dom.

"I couldn't save my boy. But if I can get the attention needed for the FBI to finally do something, then perhaps I will have contributed to saving other lives," said Mr Johnson.

Jim had a think for a moment.

"Mr Johnson, if you really want the FBI to take notice, then let me make you a better offer. Take me hostage instead," said Jim.

"As a former agent, I carry a lot more weight than that of a simple deputy, no offence, Dom," said Jim.

"None taken," said Dom.

"You'll stay?" asked Mr Johnson.

"I will, but you have to let Dom go," said Jim.

Mr Johnson thought about it for a moment. He then got up and approached the front door, then opened it a crack.

"Your deputy's coming out, but Jim is staying here with me", Mr Johnson shouted outside. He then went back into the living room.

"Go, Dom, it's okay", said Jim as Dom carefully got up and slowly went out the front door. He fast-walked down the porch and was greeted by Joey and Min, who helped him to the ambulance that had arrived.

Mr Johnson sat back down in his armchair.

"That was a very brave thing you did, Jim," said Mr Johnson.

"Well, it's been a while since I've done something like this; I have to admit I'm a little rusty", said Jim with a slight chuckle. Mr Johnson smiled a bit.

"Alex, you have to know there is still the chance that the FBI isn't going to listen to you," said Jim.

"I know, Jim, but I have to try. On my son's soul, I have to try," said Mr Johnson.

"You know, later this year, Derek would have been going to college in New York City. It'd been a dream of his for a long time. He said he was going there to learn, but I think it was mostly for the parties and pretty girls," said Mr Johnson with a chuckle.

"Well, what other reason is there to go to college?" said Jim as they both laughed.

"I know that you're probably tired of hearing this, but I do understand your pain, Alex. I know what it's like to have someone you love ripped from you," said Jim.

"Did you have a family?" asked Mr Johnson.

"No, but I really wanted one, and I nearly had it too," said Jim.

"I fell in love with this woman, and like me, she wanted a family. We both planned to run away together, and in one fell swoop, she was taken from me, as was my chance to have a family with her," said Jim.

"Is that why you quit the FBI?" asked Mr Johnson.

"Pretty much, yeah," said Jim.

"You see, I envy you, Alex. Because you actually got to have a family, a wife and a son, which is what I've wanted for a long time," said Jim.

Mr Johnson was quiet.

"I'm really not going to win this, am I, Jim?" said Mr Johnson.

"I'm afraid not," said Jim.

"Look, just come in quietly. Everyone out there knows that you're suffering; they all want to help you," said Jim.

"I shot Dom!" said Mr Johnson.

"Just a flesh wound; he's not one to hold a grudge. Let us help you, please, Alex," said Jim as Mr Johnson got up; Jim did too.

"If I give you this gun, what happens to me?" asked Mr Johnson.

"I'm afraid the Sheriff will still have to arrest you. But each of us will fight for you because you want the same thing we do: justice," said Jim as the front door opened quietly, and someone came in stealthily.

Mr Johnson turned to face Jim.

"Jim, I want you to promise me that no matter what happens, you won't stop investigating. You'll do whatever it takes to find who killed my Derek," said Mr Johnson.

"I promise you, Alex. Now, please, give me the gun," said Jim.

Mr Johnson looked at the gun in his hand for a moment.

"Okay, here you go (BANG)." Mr Johnson was suddenly shot as he tried to hand over the gun. It was Francis Morgan who'd snuck in and fired the shot.

"NO!!" Jim screamed loudly as he knelt down next to Mr Johnson, who was bleeding from his chest. Jim took off his coat and tried to staunch the bleeding.

Sheriff Hanson, Joey and Min came running in.

"What the hell happened?!" said Sheriff Hanson.

"We need help now!" said Jim.

"Joey, get Doctor Mcallister!" said Sheriff Hanson as Joey ran back out. He looked at Francis and aimed his gun at him.

"Drop it!" said Sheriff Hanson.

"What the hell are you doing?!" asked Francis.

"You heard me; drop the gun now!!" said Sheriff Hanson as Francis dropped his gun on the floor.

"Min, cuff him!" said Sheriff Hanson as Min did as he said without question.

"Hey, you can't do this; I'm a federal agent!" said Francis.

"You're about to be a bruised agent if you don't shut up; now get him out of here!" said Sheriff Hanson as Min dragged Francis out the door.

Jim remained next to Mr Johnson.

"Just hang on, Alex, help is coming," said Jim as he held his coat as tightly over the wound as he could.

Doctor Mcallister came back in with Joey and knelt down next to Mr Johnson; he checked the wound and his pulse.

"Can you do anything?" asked Jim.

Doctor Mcallister shook his head.

"He's not going to make it; there's not enough time," said Doctor Mcallister.

"Jim..." said Mr Johnson as he held up his hand; Jim held onto it.

"You're a good man, Jim...this town is grateful to have you," said Mr Johnson.

"Thank you, Mr Johnson," said Jim.

"I prefer that....it was weird when you started calling me by my first name," said Mr Johnson with a slight laugh; Jim laughed a bit too.

"But....Milford needs you....now more than ever....to find our missing people....and punish those not just for taking them....but for killing any of them," said Mr Johnson.

"It's okay, Jim....I'm going to see Derek and my wife....we're going to be a family again," said Mr Johnson.

"I'm sorry I couldn't help your son," said Jim.

"There was nothing you could do for Derek...but there's still something you can do for Tracy....she's out there....and she needs you...to find her," said Mr Johnson.

"I promise Mr Johnson, I will find Tracy, and I will punish those responsible for killing your son," said Jim.

Mr Johnson managed a small smile.

"I know you will," said Mr Johnson as he closed his eyes and fell silent.

Doctor Mcallister checked his pulse; he shook his head. Alex Johnson was dead.

Milford Sheriff's Department, Afternoon 1:25 pm

The next half hour that followed was the hardest for everyone. Alex Johnson's body was carried out by the ambulance men. Min had sent Francis ahead with another deputy and told her to lock him up in the station while she stayed behind. Min saw them carrying out Mr Johnson, her eyes filled with tears as Joey gave her a hug. The crowd that stood behind the police line to see what was happening and the deputies behind their cars all gave expressions of sadness and shock.

Jim walked out, thinking to himself about what had transpired; things were getting worse. Tracy was still missing, Derek had been murdered, and now Mr Johnson was dead. The only good news was that Dom was going to be okay; he'd been patched up and was already back at work. At the Sheriff's department, things weren't any better as Agents Lincoln and Fitzgerald were arguing with the Sheriff about Francis's incarceration.

"You have no right to lock him up; he's a federal agent!" said Fitzgerald.

"Your federal agent shot a man in cold blood, so you can bet I have every damn right to lock him up!" said Sheriff Hanson.

"He was responding to a situation; the guy had a gun in his hand!" said Lincoln.

"That "guy" was surrendering; he'd just lost his son. Jim had everything under control until Agent Morgan came charging in like John Mclane!" said Sheriff Hanson.

"We'll be informing the Director in Washington about this, that your actions are impeding a federal investigation!" said Fitzgerald.

"I await with bated breath," said Sheriff Hanson as the agents walked away.

Jim came into the station as Sheriff Hanson went over to him; he looked exhausted.

"Jim, we were wondering where you'd got to," said Sheriff Hanson.

"I just went for a walk to clear my head," said Jim.

"Jim, I hope you know that you did everything you could for Alex; what happened wasn't your fault," said Sheriff Hanson.

"I know, Sheriff. Doesn't make it any better, but thanks all the same," said Jim.

"Where's Francis?" asked Jim.

"In the lockup where I'd like to keep him forever. But his boys are already threatening to call their boss to have him released, and something tells me they mean it," said Sheriff Hanson.

"Can I talk to him?" asked Jim.

"Go right ahead," said Sheriff Hanson.

"And if there's any blood after you leave, I'll tell everyone he slipped," said Sheriff Hanson.

Jim managed a small smile as he walked away and headed for the lockup area. Francis sat there in his cell as Jim peered through the bars.

"I bet you're loving every minute of this," said Francis.

"I will admit I'm getting some sense of pleasure," said Jim.

"Well, make the most of it while it lasts. Because once Fitzgerald and Lincoln get hold of the Director, I'll be out of this shitty cell by dinnertime," said Francis.

"(scoffs) That's just like you, Francis. Always making a mess, making a phone call to the big boss to get you out of trouble and letting other people clean up your mistakes!" said Jim.

"That's not true! I was responding to a situation; I had to act in the heat of the moment!" said Francis.

"Mr Johnson was surrendering; he was handing me his gun because I'd talked him down. You had no right to fire!" said Jim.

"Well, from my angle, it looked like he was about to shoot you, and I acted to save your life!" said Francis.

"You know what, it doesn't even matter, you'll never change. But fair warning, word travels fast in this town, and I'm not going to let you hurt anyone else, you understand?!" said Jim as he started walking away. Francis got up and came right up to the bars.

"I know you still blame me for what happened five years ago. But I'm going to tell you the same thing I told you then. What happened to Agent Sandra wasn't my fault; she knew the risks going in. It was faulty intelligence that let her down, not me!" said Francis.

Jim didn't respond; he just walked away and went back into the main area.

"Well, did you slam him against the bars?" asked Sheriff Hanson.

"I was pretty tempted, but no, he's too good for that," said Jim.

"That's a shame. I was ready to shut down the lockup cameras for emergency maintenance," said Sheriff Hanson as Jim yawned.

"Jim, why don't you call it a day? Go home and rest up? You've earned it," said Sheriff Hanson.

"Yeah, yeah, maybe that's for the best. Recharge my energy cells before Francis is let off his leash," said Jim.

"I'll let you know if I hear anything," said Sheriff Hanson.

Jim smiled and nodded, then he headed out the station and went home. The Sheriff was right; it'd been a long day.

Somewhere in the Pike County Wilderness

Back at the barn, the kidnapped teens were still locked up inside. Every so often, they'd been taken away into this farmhouse across the way and tortured. It wasn't too aggressive, but the cuts and bruises spoke for themselves.

Tracy was the only one who hadn't been touched yet; she'd spent most of the day exploring the barn from top to bottom again and again. No one had really taken notice of what she'd been doing.

"Okay, Tracy, I'm going to bite; what are you doing?" asked Jimmy.

"I'm looking around," said Tracy.

"Yeah, I can see that; why are you looking around?" asked Jimmy.

"Trying to find points of interest," said Tracy.

"Oh, well, that clears it up," said Jimmy.

"Seriously, Tracy, what are you doing?" asked Cassie.

Tracy looked up higher in the loft and found a wooden ladder lying under discarded straw.

"Help me with this," said Tracy as Cassie helped her pick up the ladder and place it against the upper loft area.

"Are you going to tell me, or do we need to play Guess What all night?" asked Cassie.

"It's something that Jim taught me. You know, on one of the better days when I actually listened to him," said Tracy as she slowly climbed the ladder.

"He said that if you're trapped somewhere, whether it's by accident or forcefully, the best thing to do is explore your surroundings. Because if you look hard enough, there's always a weak spot for you to exploit" said Tracy as she got off the ladder into the loft.

"And since this barn is so old and decrepit, if we can just find enough of a weak spot in these walls, we can make a hole and escape," said Tracy, still feeling the walls. Cassie followed her up.

"I thought you said Jim would find us," said Cassie.

"He will; I'm sure he's trying his best, but there's bound to be things getting in his way. So we need a plan B in case he can't get to us in time; we need an escape plan," said Tracy.

"Sounds like Jim has taught you a lot," said Cassie.

"Yeah. He taught me a lot of things from his FBI experience or what he'd learned himself from his PI job," said Tracy as her expression dropped.

"You know, before the incident I told you about, with my mom, and then getting into that car with Leon, I told Jim that I didn't need his help because he wasn't my dad", said Tracy.

"And you want to know the worst part…..he forgave me," said Tracy.

"I mean, I've said some horrible things to him over the years, but telling someone who's looked after you that they're not your dad, it cuts deep. But Jim always forgives me too quickly, you know; sometimes I wish he'd just shout at me, scold me, tell me off, whatever," said Tracy.

"Maybe he's worried about hurting your feelings," said Cassie.

"Well, it wouldn't make any difference for all the times I've hurt him," said Tracy as she kept feeling the wall.

"Damn it, there must be a weak spot somewhere in this shitty old barn!" said Tracy.

"Tracy, just take a deep breath and calm down," said Cassie.

Tracy then looked to a corner of the barn at the back, covered by hay bales.

"Wait, I haven't checked that corner yet. Come on," said Tracy as she quickly descended the ladder and headed for the corner; Cassie followed.

"Help me move this hay," said Tracy as Cassie helped her move the hay bales. She then resumed checking the walls.

"Tracy, have you considered that maybe there isn't a way out? If this is our "holding cell", then surely those rednecks will have made sure this place is an inescapable fortress", said Cassie as Tracy tugged on some loose wood, and it started coming away, creating a hole that led to the outside.

"Then again, they're both idiots," said Cassie.

"This is great; we can make a hole big enough for all of us to squeeze through and get out of here," said Tracy as the others started running over.

"Well, what are you waiting for? Open this can of sardines, and let's bounce," said Leon.

"Wait, that's not a good idea," said Jimmy.

"Oh yeah, he's right. When we first arrived, those rednecks warned us that they're not just armed, but they also know these woods like the backs of their hands," said Tammy.

"And with those cops on their side, even if we got away from here and found a road, they'd track us down in an instant," said Jimmy.

"Right, okay then, we have to create a distraction. Something that'll blind them long enough for us to run as far as we can from them," said Tracy.

"What distraction can we do?" asked Jimmy as Tracy thought for a moment.

"I need to get into the farmhouse," said Tracy.

"Tracy, are you insane?! The only times we go into the farmhouse is when they take us in to torture us!" said Cassie.

"I need to find out what they've got in there. If they're living out here, they must have food and other supplies; maybe there's something we can use," said Tracy.

Before anyone else could speak, the doors to the barn started to open. Everyone covered the weak spot and quickly ran to different parts of the barn and sat down. Harlan and Cletus entered seconds later.

"Greetings, y'all. My boy and I have nothing to do. So I think we'd like to torture someone; how about you, Jimmy boy?" said Harlan.

"Oh, come on, you've gone at him hard enough already!" said Tammy.

Cletus approached Jimmy, but Tracy suddenly got up.

"Take me instead!" said Tracy.

"Ha, I see what you're trying to do, Tracy, but it doesn't work that way. Now sit back down," said Harlan.

"No," said Tracy.

"I beg your pardon?" said Harlan.

"I said no," said Tracy.

"Tracy, you may not think much of me and my boy, but we have some degree of respect. Now do as you're told and sit down!" said Harlan.

"Eat shit!" said Tracy.

"Cletus!" said Harlan as Cletus grabbed hold of Tracy.

"You've just lost one of your chances, Tracy, and for that, you'll be punished. Take her inside, Cletus!" said Harlan as Cletus marched Tracy out.

"Hey, wait!" said Leon as he tried to go after her, but Harlan cocked his shotgun and aimed at him.

"Unless you really want to see your insides, rich boy, sit your ass down!" said Harlan as Leon did what he said. Harlan left the barn, then closed and locked the doors.

Harlan and Cletus led Tracy over what was a big open yard area to the farmhouse across the way; she kept scanning around for anything of note as they walked.

Finally, they entered the farmhouse. Inside, it looked as dilapidated and falling apart as the barn; not even an interior designer from one of those TV shows could save this place. Tracy found herself in a wide entranceway with a staircase leading to another floor; on either side were two doorways, one leading to a living room and the other leading to what looked like a kitchen, that caught Tracy's interest.

Harlan and Cletus took Tracy down some stairs that led to a basement. Harlan opened a big metal door before they entered; he then closed and locked it behind them. The basement was surprisingly small; a wooden chair with a single light above it and two tables with trays of various knives and sharpened blades were down there. Cletus took Tracy over to the chair and strapped down her wrists with two metal cuffs attached to the chair.

"This place is a bit cliched, isn't it?" said Tracy.

"Say what?" asked Cletus.

"Well, the wooden chair with the cuffs on the arms, the single shaking light above me and the knives and other torture devices. This is like something out of a cheap horror movie," said Tracy.

"That's what we're going for, girly," said Cletus.

"And for the record, I like cheap horror movies," said Cletus.

"I'm sure a lot's going through your head, Tracy, like how two respectable people got involved in something like this", said Harlan.

"The thought had crossed my mind," said Tracy.

"Well, me and Cletus didn't have much else to do. After we lost our farm to the goddamn taxman, we were struggling to find a place to call home," said Harlan.

"Then we found this place; it was abandoned when we arrived, so we just took it," said Cletus.

"So, how did the cops find you?" asked Tracy.

"Through our criminal records, if you must know. Oh, we didn't do anything too bad, some vandalism, couple thefts, few fights that were technically self-defence, but the cops round here are racist to us rednecks. Anyway, those two guys found us and made an offer," said Harlan.

"It was one we couldn't refuse," said Cletus.

"So they're paying you guys?" asked Tracy as Harlan and Cletus laughed.

"As I told Cassie before, we're not in this for the money; we just want to have fun," said Harlan.

"The cops said we could do as we pleased with whoever they brought us. "Have as much fun as possible", they said," said Cletus.

"So those cops are kidnapping people off the road, then bringing them to you guys just so you can have fun?!" said Tracy.

"Exhilarating, isn't it?" said Cletus as he started feeling Tracy's hair.

"You got very pretty hair; I like blonde ones. Can I sniff it?" said Cletus.

"You know what else is blonde, a lama? Why don't you go sniff that?" said Tracy.

"I tried that once…..he didn't like it very much," said Cletus.

"Now then, Tracy, since this is your first time and despite you breaking one of your chances, I'll give you the luxury of deciding. Who do you want to go first, myself or the boy?" said Harlan as he stood there with a sharpened cleaver, and Cletus stood opposite with a sharpened hunting knife; both of them had creepy smiles.

Deep down, Tracy was scared stiff, but despite all that, she had to remain strong for as long as possible, so she made her choice.

Chapter 14
A Friend in Trouble

Milford Sheriff's Department: Evening 9:30 pm

The agents approached Sheriff Hanson with a piece of paper that had come straight from the Director of the FBI. With a big sigh, he read it and looked at Min.

"Let him out," said Sheriff Hanson.

Min knew roughly what that paper had said and what the agent's smiles signified.

"Yes, Sheriff," said Min with some disappointment as she led the agents to the lockup and opened the cell door. She left quickly as Francis walked out and stretched his arms.

"What took you guys so long?" asked Francis.

"Well, we thought we'd give you a while so we could find out what they serve for dinner around here," said Lincoln.

"Did you find what we were looking for?" asked Francis.

"That and better," said Fitzgerald as he handed what looked like a phone transcript to Francis; he smiled.

"Gentlemen, we're paying Deputy Brandon a visit," said Francis.

Jim Gold's House, Evening 9:42 pm

Jim had made it home, and shortly after getting in, he sat down on the couch and passed out. He was happily asleep with no nightmares.

"(knock, knock) Jim, Jim, are you in there, Jim? Wake up, please!" suddenly, some frantic knocking at the front door and the sound of Joey shouting in a panicked voice broke the silence and woke him up.

Jim went for the front door and opened it as Joey was still frantically knocking and shouting to let him in.

"Jim, close the door, lock it!" said Joey as he ran inside and closed the living room curtains. Jim closed and locked the door with some confusion. He went into the living room to find Joey pacing and sweating.

"Joey, what's happening?" asked Jim.

"They're after me, Jim, the FBI are after me!" said Joey.

"Whoa, Joey, calm down, just breathe and tell me what's happening," said Jim.

Joey tried to breathe, but he couldn't stay calm.

"The Sheriff had to release Francis from the cells since the Director sent a threatening document telling him to do so. I'd only just gone home before it happened, a long day, as you know. Anyway, Francis then shows up outside my front door and says they need to talk to me, but before I can reach for the door handle, he suddenly says that they have a warrant for my arrest!" said Joey.

"Why? You haven't done anything wrong!" said Jim.

"I know, don't you think I know! Anyway, I panicked; I bolted out the back door and came to you," said Joey.

"You got to hide me, Jim, whatever they're trying to accuse me of, I didn't do it!" said Joey.

"Look, Joey, just stay calm, and we'll figure this-(knock, knock)" Jim was interrupted by more knocking at the front door.

"Jim Gold, it's Francis Morgan," said Francis.

"He's found me!" Joey whispered.

Francis knocked a few more times and announced his presence. Jim ushered Joey to be quiet.

"Out the back", Jim whispered as he and Joey started quietly approaching the back door to the yard, which also had a gate that led to the street.

As they reached the back, Francis announced that he was going to count to three and then kick the door down. Jim and Joey snuck out and closed the back door.

"Go, go," said Jim quietly as Joey ran across the yard and out the back gate.

Jim watched Francis kick the front door in and start looking around with his gun out. Jim quickly headed for the back gate but stopped before going through it. Something was wrong; it was too quiet.

"Joey, I'm coming out!" Jim loudly announced before heading out the gate.

Seconds after, Jim quickly ducked down as someone swung for him; he delivered a punch back, which hit what turned out to be Agent Fitzgerald. Agent Lincoln was there too; he had hold of Joey but let him go and swung for Jim, who grabbed him by the arm and flipped him over. Suddenly, a gunshot tore a hole in the wooden fence; Jim looked back to see it was Francis in the backyard.

"Joey, run, go!" said Jim.

"No, stick around, Joey. Don't you want to know if my next shot will miss as well?" said Francis as he approached Jim.

"You wouldn't dare, Francis!" said Jim.

"Wouldn't I? You were helping a potential suspect to escape, and you just assaulted two FBI agents. Who's to say that any wounds you sustained were only because I was doing my job?" said Francis.

"Sheriff Hanson will never believe you," said Jim.

"Maybe not. But then again, he's not my boss," said Francis.

Fitzgerald and Lincoln started getting up.

"You boys okay?" asked Francis.

"We'll be fine, sir. He pulled a switch, caught us off guard instead of him," said Fitzgerald.

"Well, couldn't have expected you to have forgotten all your FBI training, could we?" said Francis as he turned to face Joey.

"Joey, Deputy Brandon, why did you run, man? We just wanted to talk to you," said Francis.

"You said you had a warrant for my arrest, and I haven't done anything wrong!" said Joey.

"Isn't that for us to decide? Look, don't make this any harder, Joey; just come with us, and we'll have ourselves a nice chat," said Francis.

"I don't trust you," said Joey.

"Alright then, maybe a little incentive then. Restrain him (points at Jim)," said Francis as Fitzgerald and Lincoln grabbed and restrained Jim.

"What are you doing?!" asked Joey.

"Incentive, like I said," said Francis as he turned and started punching Jim twice in the stomach, three times in the face.

"STOP, just stop!" shouted Joey.

"Okay, you psycho, I'll come quietly; just stop hurting him!" said Joey as Francis stopped.

"Fitz, cuff him," said Francis as Fitzgerald cuffed Joey.

"What about Jim?" asked Lincoln.

"We'll drop his ass off at the clinic on the way; give him time to do some thinking," said Francis as they walked Joey and dragged Jim to their car.

Milford Sheriff's Department, Evening 9:50 pm

The shock on everyone's faces when the FBI marched into the station with Joey handcuffed, cannot be described. Sheriff

Hanson was quick to jump into action and block their path. A few other deputies joined him.

"What's the meaning of this?!" asked Sheriff Hanson.

"Deputy Brandon is under arrest by order of the FBI," said Francis.

"Sherriff, this guy's out of his mind! He beat up Jim right in front of me just to make me surrender!" said Joey.

"Is that true?" asked Sheriff Hanson.

"I only gave him a couple of taps; it's not like I broke any bones. We dropped him off at the clinic, and Doctor Mcallister said he was going to be fine," said Francis.

"You think that because you're some big shot agent on an important mission, that you can just go around shooting people and beating them up? Not in my town!" said Sheriff Hanson.

"Well, you're right on two counts, Sheriff. Yes, I'm an important agent, and yes, I'm on a mission to find a very important person. Someone we should have found days ago if not for your continued non-cooperation!" said Francis.

"On what charge are you arresting Joey?" asked Sheriff Hanson.

"Well, here's where it gets a bit complicated, so here goes. The truth is that the FBI has known about these disappearances in Pike County and has been secretly investigating them for a while. And now, thanks to the results we got back from the lab, we finally have a suspect, a county cop by the name of Frank Boles," said Francis.

"His fingerprints were on the driver's side door, and his shoe print was on the back of the car," said Francis.

"And according to our search, not only was Frank in town a few days ago, but he's also old high school friends with Joey here," said Francis.

"What does that prove? So if I have a best friend I haven't spoken to since kindergarten, and now he's the worst serial killer in the whole nation, am I going to be arrested just because we used to play hopscotch?!" said Sheriff Hanson.

"There's a difference in the matter, Sheriff. You see, we've been wondering for a while, how did Officer Boles know which cars to target? How did he know which ones had the teenagers inside? Unless he had help. And according to this phone transcript taken from the night Leon Thornberg went missing, a call was made to Officer Boles using an unregistered number, and look at whose phone it was traced back to," said Francis as he handed the transcript to Sheriff Hanson, he read it and saw Francis was right.

"Sheriff, it's a mistake; I swear I didn't do anything!" said Joey.

"Of course, you didn't do it, Joey; it's obvious you're being set up. It's just a shame Mr Big Shot agent can't see that," said Sheriff Hanson.

"If you have evidence to counteract this, Sheriff, then you best show me now," said Francis.

Everyone was quiet.

"Thought so. Joey Brandon is to remain in custody, pending further interrogation; take him to the cell," said Francis as the agents started walking Joey away. But the other deputies, including Min, wouldn't move out of their path.

"Sheriff, this is getting tiresome. I've tried to put up with your non cooperation, but my patience is running thin. Now, if you like, I can put in a call to the Director and have him send down twenty more agents to take over this station and clear everyone out. Is that what it's going to take?!" said Francis.

"Sheriff, it's okay," said Joey.

Sheriff Hanson was quiet; he then gently waved his arm for the deputies to clear a path. Min approached Joey.

"This isn't fair!" said Min.

"No, it isn't," said Joey.

"We're going to find out what's happening, Joey; we won't let this slide!" said Sheriff Hanson.

Joey smiled as he also received a kiss on the cheek from Min.

"We won't let you down," said Min.

"I know you won't," said Joey as the agents pushed him forward and into the holding area; Francis followed.

"Min, go to Jim's house and check at the clinic, find out if that bastard was telling the truth about him," said Sheriff Hanson.

"Yes, Sheriff," said Min as she raced out of the station.

"Dom, work with Eric and Karen. Get me phone transcripts of every call made from this station in the last month, including mine; now get to it!" said Sheriff Hanson.

"On it, Sheriff," said Dom as he walked away to carry out the task.

"Joey, you....damn it, I'll...find out what I can about Frank Boles," said Sheriff Hanson as he walked away.

Things were now more tense than ever, and no one knew if it'd get better or worse.

Somewhere in the Pike County Wilderness

Everyone was waiting anxiously in the barn; Tracy had been gone for the last couple of hours. Finally, the doors unlocked and opened as Cletus came in with Tracy and threw her inside; he then quickly closed and locked the door as Leon ran to Tracy, the others joined in.

"Tracy, babe, are you okay?" asked Leon.

Tracy had a few cuts to her hands and her face, but nothing big or life-threatening.

"I thought I told you to stop calling me babe," said Tracy.

"Well, I was worried about you," said Leon.

"So, was it worth it? Did you find what you were looking for?" asked Cassie. Tracy smiled.

"I think I have a plan, but I need to get back into the farmhouse. Here's what you guys need to do," said Tracy.

Milford Clinic, the next morning 8:00 am

Jim was lying in a small bed in one of the rooms at the clinic; he was looking around the room with blurry eyesight and slow breathing. Then Jim heard a voice.

"Jim, over here, Jim," said a woman's voice.

Jim turned to see someone sitting in the chair next to his bed. It was a woman with brunette hair and a beautiful face.

"Matilda?" said Jim.

"Hey Jim, you look like you've been through the wringer," said Matilda.

"What, what are you doing here?" asked Jim.

"I came to see you, silly; it's been so lonely here without you," said Matilda.

"I'm sorry...I'm sorry....I couldn't save you," said Jim.

"It's okay, Jim, it wasn't your fault. Besides, I'm not alone anymore; I have someone to keep me company," said Matilda as she pointed to the front of the bed; a figure standing there became Tracy Kean.

"Hey Jim, it's me, Tracy," said Tracy.

"Tracy....wait...you can't be here," said Jim.

"I am; I'm with Matilda now, keeping her company. She's really funny," said Tracy.

"Wait...no, this...this isn't right...you're not dead, Tracy...you're not," said Jim.

"We're here, Jim, the both of us. We're waiting for you to join us; you know you want to," said Matilda.

"No...Tracy....she's not dead...she's not....I have to find her....I'll find you, Tracy....no...don't go!" said Jim as he suddenly opened his eyes. He was still in the bed, sweating and breathing heavily; it'd all been a dream.

He looked around the room and found Min was resting on the clinic armchair with her jacket as a cover.

"Min, Min!" said Jim a bit weakly; Min woke up.

"Jim, sorry," said Min.

"Sleeping on the job?" said Jim.

"Nah, I'm off the clock. How are you?" said Min while stretching.

"I'm okay, a bit sore in places, but I've had worse....I didn't dream about Joey, did I?" said Jim.

"I'm afraid not. Agent Morgan marched him through the station in handcuffs in front of everyone. He basically said he was a traitor, helping Frank Boles to kidnap people," said Min.

"Officer Frank Boles, his old school friend?" asked Jim.

"Yeah, and get this, the FBI has known these disappearances were actually kidnappings for a while, but they didn't tell us," said Min.

"How is Joey supposed to have helped Officer Boles?" asked Jim.

"Agent Morgan acquired a phone transcript; he said that someone was calling Frank over the last month from the station and telling him which cars to target. And the calls apparently came from Joey's phone," said Min.

"Goddamn it, Francis!" said Jim.

"Joey said Francis beat you up to force him to surrender?" asked Min.

"Yeah, he's lucky his henchmen were there; otherwise, he would have been the one in the clinic", said Jim. Min smiled a bit.

"So what's Francis got planned next?" asked Jim.

"He didn't say; he already threatened to call more agents and evict us if we keep getting in his way. Joey is yet to be questioned, though" said Min.

"I need to talk to Joey; he might know something about how he's being set up or why him," said Jim as he tried to get up.

"Jim, you need to keep still. Doctor Mcallister said he did what he could, but you still need a few more hours of bedrest before moving," said Min.

"Min, this may surprise you, but I once went one-on-one with a Colombian drug baron who was a professional wrestler in an earlier life. Despite the fact he basically handed my ass to me, I still took him down, and then I was in and out of the hospital within a day, walking around as if nothing had happened," said Jim.

"Francis is basically the mouse fighting the cat; I'll be alright," said Jim.

"That may be, but at least wait a few more hours before doing anything drastic," said Min.

"(sigh) Okay then," said Jim as he laid back down.

There was a knock at the door, and as it opened, Doctor Mcallister and Sheriff Hanson walked into the room.

"Ah, Mr Gold, how are we feeling this morning?" asked Doctor Mcallister.

"I'm still a bit sore in places, but otherwise, I'm doing good Doc," said Jim.

"Well, that's good to hear; when they brought you here last night, you were in quite a state. I did everything I could and took some X-rays. As far as I can tell, two to three more hours and you can try walking around, but something tells me you'll be up and at them before we know it," said Doctor Mcallister.

"Now, there is one thing I'd like to discuss, but maybe it'd be better without an audience," said Doctor Mcallister.

"Do you want us to step out for a minute?" asked Sheriff Hanson.

"If it's okay with you, Sheriff," said Jim.

"Come on, Min, I'll get you some coffee," said Sheriff Hanson as he left the room with Min.

"What's wrong, Doc? Why did they have to leave?" asked Jim.

"Because there's something I found that I'm a little concerned about; let me show you", said Doctor Mcallister as he showed Jim some imaging from a brain scan.

"I had to do a brain scan to make sure you didn't have any sort of head trauma from the assault. Now, thankfully, you don't, but I was a little worried about your mental state. The recordings were off the charts, and you were exhibiting signs of trauma while sleeping. So Jim, I have to ask, have you had any sort of mental trauma or PTSD that you haven't told us about?" said Doctor Mcallister.

Jim thought about it for a moment. He could have lied, but Doctor Mcallister was like the Sheriff; he could always tell a lie from the truth.

"Five years ago, a woman I cared about in the FBI was killed during an undercover operation. We were really close, and her sudden death hit me hard," said Jim.

"Do you suffer from nightmares?" asked Doctor Mcallister.

"I used to, a lot after it happened. Things have actually been better the last few years since I moved to Milford. But recent events seem to have brought them back," said Jim.

"I see, and I'm going to hazard a guess that you haven't sought out treatment?" asked Doctor Mcallister.

"No, like I said, when I moved down here, things got better. I didn't think I needed to," said Jim.

"Jim, I may seem like just a small-town doctor, but I've seen these types of things before. Mostly from people who moved here or even if they're just passing through town," said Doctor Mcallister.

"Ex-cops, retired war vets, I've even had some of the locals in here, like Alex Johnson," said Doctor Mcallister.

"Mr Johnson had trauma?" asked Jim.

"After he lost his wife, yes. He'd never admit it, but he was hit pretty hard, and at one point, he was worried about becoming a threat to his son," said Doctor Mcallister.

"Jim, you are your own man and more than capable of making your own decisions. But take some medical advice and sign up for treatment; I'm not suggesting chemicals, but maybe some therapy. Talk to a person about it; I even have a friend who can help; she's really good at her job," said Doctor Mcallister.

"Once Tracy is safely home and the kidnappings have stopped, then I'll consider it", said Jim.

"Let's just hope it's not too late by then", said Doctor Mcallister as he left the room.

Sheriff Hanson and Min were waiting outside with their coffee cups. They came inside shortly after he left.

"All good?" asked Sheriff Hanson.

"Reasonably good. So, what's the next step?" said Jim.

"Well, I've got Dom, Eric and Karen gathering all the station's phone transcripts from the last month. If Joey's name appears on any more calls made with that unregistered number, it'll further support our theory that he's being set up," said Sheriff Hanson.

"I was also going to look into Officer Boles's history. Then I got a phone call from your FBI friend Dylan, who says you asked him to do the same a while ago," said Sheriff Hanson.

"He says he's sorry, but he's still really busy with a drug case. We've decided that we're going to put our heads together and see what we can each dig up on the guy," said Sheriff Hanson.

"As for Joey, all we can do is make sure he's comfortable and keep watch when Agent Morgan questions him," said Min.

"Any leads on Tracy or the other missing teens?" asked Jim.

Sheriff Hanson shook his head.

"Afraid not, I've called the Pike County Police, and they say they're still looking into it. But given that Officer Boles is one of them, he probably knows how to cover his tracks," said Sheriff Hanson.

"We'll find something, Jim, we haven't given up," said Min as Jim smiled a bit.

"Oh, in the meantime, this might interest you", said Sheriff Hanson as he handed a big brown envelope to Jim.

"What's this?" asked Jim as he opened the letter and pulled out some documents.

"Remember Todd Hunter's stolen money? The lab finally got back on those prints we lifted from his safe. They apologise for the delay, but as expected, it wasn't very high on their priority list," said Sheriff Hanson.

Jim read the documents, and his eyes widened.

"Are these accurate?" asked Jim.

"I had a look myself; I'm afraid it's true," said Sheriff Hanson.

Jim was shocked by what he saw, but one thing was clear: he now knew who the thief was.

Chapter 15
Painful Admissions and Cunning Plans

Todd Hunter's General Store, Morning 11:05 am

The Violet Show broadcasted at 9:00 am.

"Good morning Milford, you're listening to the Violet Show. I'm your host, Violet, and we've got some news for you, but it's not good, I'm afraid. My uncle, the Sheriff, just informed me that Deputy Joey Brandon has just been arrested in connection to the supposed kidnappings in Pike County. This is, of course, infuriating as we all know the kind of man that Joey is: a good man with a good heart. And not only that but our resident PI, Jim Gold, was hospitalised in the clinic while trying to defend Joey from the FBI. I know that everyone would be more than willing to run those FBI guys out of town, but we must stay calm and resist the urge to riot. In the meantime, we must all show our support for Joey and pray for our favourite PI to get well soon," said Violet over the radio.

Jim left the clinic after being able to get up and walk after three hours; he then went to the General Store. He was still piecing together what he'd read in the report and couldn't believe who the prints led to. One thing was certain, though: Jim needed to get answers before Todd became wise and found out himself, and then there'd be hell to pay.

Jim entered the General Store and faced who the thief was.

"Hello, Gomez," said Jim.

"Jim, hi, I heard what happened to you on the Violet Show. Are you okay?" said Gomez after putting something on the shelf.

"I'm good, Gomez, thank you for asking. There's something I was hoping to talk to you about," said Jim.

"Of course, do you have news of Tracy?" said Gomez.

"No, I'm afraid not. Um, is there somewhere more private we can talk?" said Jim.

"Uh, sure, we can talk in the storeroom in the back; follow me", said Gomez as he led Jim to the back storeroom and let him in first.

"I'm taking five minutes, Mr Hunter; Jim needs to talk to me", said Gomez to Todd, standing behind the counter.

"Alright, kid," said Todd as Gomez went inside and closed the door.

"So what's up, Jim?" asked Gomez.

"Why did you take Todd Hunter's money?" asked Jim.

"What?" asked Gomez.

"Gomez, I've known you long enough; please don't play the idiot with me," said Jim.

"The forensic lab finally got back to us on that set of fingerprints from Todd Hunter's safe; they match you, Gomez. You may have been wearing gloves, but you were gripping the lock so hard your prints came through the fabric," said Jim.

"And the bolt cutters that were used to cut the padlock, they were a special pair that's only sold in the store" said Jim.

Gomez was quiet, and he started pacing. Jim recognised the look on his face; he knew he'd been found out.

"Have you told Mr Hunter?" asked Gomez.

"No, not yet. I wanted to hear it from you first," said Jim.

Gomez still didn't seem sure.

"Gomez, why would you do this? Todd's been nothing but nice to you; he gave you a job, and he treats you like his son!" said Jim.

"He's been nice to me, he gave me a job, he treats me like his son". All is true except for the last bit, Jim. Try "Treats me like his son until you actually want something from him" How about that?!" said Gomez.

"Was that what this was all about? Wanting money?" asked Jim.

"No, I mean yes, but…Jim, whatever you're thinking, this has nothing to do with gambling or women, okay, nothing like that!" said Gomez.

"Then tell me what it is," said Jim.

Gomez looked like he was about to cry when he answered.

"Jim….my mom's dying," said Gomez.

That surprised Jim as he didn't expect to hear it.

"Miss Salazer? What is it?" asked Jim.

"Kidney failure. She went for a routine checkup two months ago; that was when they found it," said Gomez.

"The doctors said it was pretty bad since they'd discovered it late. But there was still a chance to do a kidney transplant, only...it required a very expensive operation," said Gomez.

"How much is it?" asked Jim.

"Let's just say the amount it costs would be enough for my mother and me to go on a Mediterranean Cruise, buy things from all the gift shops, and still have a bit left over by the time we get back," said Gomez.

"So, you went to Todd and asked him for the money to pay for it?" asked Jim.

"Not the whole amount. My mom had some money saved for a rainy day, and I had my wages built up from the time I worked here, but the final amount was what I asked Mr Hunter for. I explained the situation, but he told me that he couldn't afford it," said Gomez.

"Can you believe it? He was sitting on over two hundred thousand dollars, and he couldn't spare any of it to help my mom!" said Gomez.

"How did you know about the money or that he had a safe?" asked Jim.

"A couple of years ago, Mr Hunter got drunk at Shaw's and worried about him driving home in that state, I offered to take him. During the ride, he started laughing about having a big secret, then he told me about the safe and the money he was putting in there; the amount was lower back then," said Gomez.

"But when he told you that he couldn't give you any money towards the operation, you snapped," said Jim.

"It wasn't like that; I was upset, Jim; my mom's all I have left. But when Mr Hunter refused to help me, I decided there was only one thing I could do," said Gomez.

"So I snuck onto his property that night, used some bolt cutters from the store to get past the padlock to the shed, then found the safe exactly where he told me it'd be", said Gomez.

"How did you get past the combination lock?" asked Jim.

"It actually wasn't that hard. You know there's a reason they tell people not to make combinations and passwords on their birthday," said Gomez.

"Gomez, forgive me, but I have to ask. Where is Todd's money?" said Jim.

"Gone, every penny of it. I gave it to my mom's doctor to finalise the payment; he's booked her operation for tomorrow," said Gomez.

"I see," said Jim.

"Jim, I don't normally do things like this, but you have to believe me, I did it for my mom!" said Gomez.

"Gomez, it's okay, I understand. If it'd been my mother, I probably would've done the same thing," said Jim.

"But if Todd finds out, he won't just fire you; he'll be out for your blood; you took his nest egg", said Jim.

"I know, and no amount of saying sorry or promising to pay it back will ever make up for what I did. Jim, you can't tell him, please, you can't, he'll want to hang me from a rope, please, don't tell him!" said Gomez.

Jim could see how frightened Gomez was; he fully understood he did it to save his mother. But Todd was expecting an answer, and Jim had no choice but to give him one.

Jim opened the storeroom door.

"Todd, can you come in here for a minute?" asked Jim.

"Uh, yeah, sure," said Todd as he left the counter and came into the storeroom.

"What's going on here?" asked Todd.

"I believe that Gomez has something he'd like to tell you," said Jim.

"Jim, please" Gomez whispered.

"It's okay, Gomez. I'm sure Todd will understand how you were threatened to reveal his safe location by a professional thief," said Jim.

Gomez was almost as surprised as Todd.

"What?" asked Todd.

"I know who took your money, Todd, and it wasn't old man Wilson; in fact, it wasn't a local at all. I'm sorry to say that you were the target of a professional thief looking to keep his skills sharpened by committing small acts of larceny wherever he went," said Jim.

"So, some random thief stole my money?" asked Todd.

"A professional thief" said Jim.

"But how did he know about my safe, and where does Gomez fit into this?" asked Todd.

"Gomez, do you want to tell Todd how you knew about his safe?" asked Jim.

"A couple of years ago, I drove you home after you got drunk in Shaw's. You unknowingly told me everything about your safe and the money you kept in there. I promised myself I'd keep it a secret," said Gomez.

"When the thief discovered that Gomez had knowledge of the safe, he threatened the poor kid and even used his mother as leverage, forcing him to reveal everything he knew," said Jim.

"Wait, you said I told you that two years ago? Why did the thief wait so long to strike?" asked Todd.

"Because he's a busy man, Todd is always looking for his next prize, the next job. He had a contact in town who found out about the safe, but with it being a small theft, it wasn't very high on the priority list," said Jim.

"So he bided his time and waited until he was short on money again. Then, he came to town, forced the information out of Gomez, and helped himself to your retirement fund," said Jim.

"So where's the thief now?" asked Todd.

"He's gone, Todd, vanished into the wind, your money too," said Jim.

Todd didn't look happy.

"Well….it's not the outcome I was expecting. But at least I know that's something," said Todd.

"I'm really sorry, Mr Hunter," said Gomez.

"Don't apologise, Gomez; I'm sorry that I put you in that position; it was never my intention", said Todd.

"And I'm sorry I couldn't help your mother either," said Todd.

"Oh, it's okay; Mother's got her operation booked for tomorrow," said Gomez.

"Really? I thought you said you couldn't afford the remainder of the price?" asked Todd.

Gomez froze as it felt like everything was about to be undone.

"It was a charitable donation from an anonymous donor," said Jim.

Todd didn't say anything for a moment, then he smiled.

"I guess no matter where you are, there are always good people to be found out there," said Todd.

"I'm happy for you and your mother, Gomez," said Todd.

"Thank you, Mr Hunter" said Gomez.

"I presume you'll be wanting the day off tomorrow to go with your mother," said Todd.

"If that's okay with you, Mr Hunter," said Gomez.

"Of course, it's okay. Now come on, kid, let's get back to work," said Todd as he opened the door.

"Yes, Mr Hunter," said Gomez as he left the room.

"I'm sorry to have wasted your time on this, Jim," said Todd.

"It's okay, Todd; I was happy to help," said Jim.

"I should give you payment, but I don't know if I can afford your price at the moment," said Todd.

"This one's on the house," said Jim.

Todd smiled and left the room, then went back behind the counter. Jim left, too and headed for the exit; he looked back at Gomez, who silently mouthed, "Thank you." Jim just smiled and left the store. The case had reached a conclusion; now, he could focus all his attention on the big one, finding Tracy.

Somewhere in the Pike County Wilderness

At the farm, Tracy had explained the plan to everyone, and they were all ready to put it into action. The plan involved creating a distraction so that Tracy could sneak into the farmhouse and find what she needed for the escape.

Tracy had torn a bigger hole in the side of the barn to get out. They'd covered it up again for the next step, which involved Leon.

"I can't believe I agreed to this," said Leon.

"Don't be such a little bitch, be a man" said Jimmy.

"Yeah, take one for the team," said Tammy.

"I'm doing this for you, Tracy, only you," said Leon.

"Leon....I really appreciate this," said Tracy.

Leon smiled a bit as he approached the door to the barn, and then he started shouting and kicking the door.

"HEY, HEY, YEAH, I'M TALKING TO YOU, HILLBILLIES, LET ME OUT OF HERE, COME ON, LET ME OUT, HILLBILLIES!!!" shouted Leon as loud as he could.

No sooner had he done it than Cletus and Harlan approached the barn; they unlocked the door and stepped inside.

"Will you stop shouting so loud, boy? You damn near burst my eardrums!" said Cletus.

"I want out of this place; I can't take anymore, you damn dirty hillbilly!" said Leon.

"Now you shut your mouth! Describing me and my Pa as hillbillies is a discriminatory comment," said Cletus.

"Discriminatory, Cletus," said Harlan.

"Yeah, that too," said Cletus.

"Me and my Pa are rednecks, plain and simple. I think you'll find between hillbillies and rednecks, there's a deference," said Cletus.

"Difference, Cletus," said Harlan.

"Yeah, that too!" said Cletus.

"Now, are you going to apologise for your hurtful comments?" asked Cletus.

"You want an apology? Here's my apology!" said Leon as he suddenly punched Cletus in the face.

Harlan aimed his shotgun at the others.

"Don't move!" said Harlan.

"He hit me Pa!" said Cletus.

"Stop blubbering, boy and take him inside!" said Harlan as Cletus got up, hit Leon in the stomach, then grabbed him and marched him out of the barn; Harlan followed and locked the doors.

"Give them a moment to get inside," said Tracy as Tammy and Jimmy watched through the cracks. They waited for the rednecks to enter the farmhouse with Leon.

"They're inside," said Tammy.

"Here goes everything," said Tracy as she climbed through the hole.

"Good luck," said Cassie as she did.

Tracy climbed out into the yard, crouched down, and started to make her way across the yard as quietly as she could. The squelching sound of stepping in the mud was unfortunate, but thankfully, it wasn't a giveaway. Tracy reached the front door and peered through the keyhole; the hallway was empty. She took the risk and quietly opened the front door, then stepped inside.

Tracy quietly closed the door behind her and stopped for a moment to listen; she could hear the sounds of Harlan and Cletus's laughs from the basement. She hated using Leon as bait, but it was the only way to keep them distracted long enough for her to get what she needed, so long as they didn't get bored too quickly.

Tracy snuck into the kitchen and started to check through the drawers and cupboards as quietly as she could. She found various food and drink items which confirmed the redneck's story about living there. Tracy kept searching until she found a cupboard of glasses; she took a tall one and placed it on the counter; she then opened a drawer filled with an assortment of tape, plastic, scissors and a few small lids to cover the top of the glasses. Tracy took one of the lids and carefully snipped off a piece of tape, then used it to stick the lid on. More searching then caused Tracy to quietly say "Yes!" to herself as she'd found some unmixed lemon juice, perfect for what she had planned; she took the box, opened the glass and poured a medium amount into it, then put the box back in its place.

Another drawer that Tracy opened was filled with cutlery. She still wasn't sure about Jimmy's plan, but she took one of the smaller knives, knowing it would be easier to conceal and placed it in her pocket.

Tracy closed and restuck the lid, then she quietly said, "Now, Jim said a capsule was all it would require." She looked around and saw what looked like a small laundry room next to the kitchen.

"That's the most likely place," Tracy said to herself as she went back to crouch mode and crept inside. The room just had one washing machine and one dryer, and then Tracy found what she was looking for a packet of laundry capsules stuck between the two machines. Tracy looked around and tried to remove it quietly; she managed to loosen it enough that she was able to reach inside and pull out a single capsule; she then put the box back in its place.

Tracy returned to the kitchen after placing the capsule in her pocket, then she grabbed the glass of lemon juice and held onto it.

Tracy decided it was time to get out of there. But as she headed for the door, voices could still be heard from the basement.

"You guys really don't know anything; I bet you can't even read!" said Leon.

"You shut your damn mouth, boy, I can read just fine. I've been learning how to read a map; it's in my room upstairs if you'd like to see it," said Cletus.

"He doesn't want to see your bad map reading Cletus. The last time I took directions from you, we both fell into the lake," said Harlan.

"The map said we had to walk through it to get to the other side," said Cletus.

Now Tracy was struck with a new thought: a map would be very useful to determine, at the very least, an approximation of where they might be. It was risky, though; it meant climbing the stairs and finding the room of the redneck called Cletus.

Tracy gulped as she headed for the stairs. She put one foot on the step, and it creaked; she stopped and waited; thankfully, it seemed no one heard it as there was still laughing below. She then remembered another trick that Jim had taught her; she started to tiptoe up the stairs by standing on the edge of each step and avoiding the board part; it worked; Tracy reached the top of the stairs with no problems. Now she had another issue: a long corridor with two doors at either end; which one was the room with the map?

Tracy crept forward carefully and tried to look at the doors; she then saw something that made her sigh, a very obvious sign that said, "Cletus's Room, don't y'all enter now!". Tracy shook her head and quietly approached the room; she opened the door and went inside. The room wasn't very nice, just as dilapidated as the rest of the house, with only a small bed, a walk-in wardrobe, a shady window and a small table which had the map on it. Tracy crept to the table and started looking at the map of the Pike County region, which is what she was hoping for. Tracy started looking it over until she found Milford, then she followed the road she and Leon took and tried to figure out where they could be, then she saw something.

"The Marston Homestead is quite a distance from where Leon and I were, an hour to get there and completely secluded from any roads," said Tracy quietly.

She then took down the map coordinates on a piece of paper and tore it from the notepad on the table; luckily, it didn't look obvious that a page was missing. Tracy turned to leave, but she heard something that made her heart start to beat at a mile a minute: footsteps coming towards the room. Tracy had to think quickly; she crept to the walk-in wardrobe and hid inside. Cletus came into the room and folded the map on the table.

"I can read a map as well as the next guy; I'll show that little rich prick!" said Cletus as he headed out of the room.

Tracy was about to sigh with relief when she pressed her foot down and made the board under her creak; she quickly placed her hand over her mouth as Cletus came back in. He looked around a bit and came very close to the wardrobe; Tracy just kept silent. Finally, Cletus shook his head and left the room; Tracy silently exhaled.

After waiting a moment to hear Cletus going down the stairs, Tracy emerged from the wardrobe and crept out of the room; she followed the corridor and tiptoed back down the stairs. She could hear the sound of Cletus arguing with Leon about map reading as she crept out of the front door. With the glass she'd placed in her pocket, she checked to make sure it hadn't leaked; it was still in the glass. Tracy smiled a bit as she was about to head for the barn, then she noticed something: her footprints approaching the house were very clear on the muddy ground. She was then close to having a panic attack when she heard the sound of Harlan and Cletus exiting the basement with Leon. She didn't know what to do, then the unthinkable happened.

Thunder clapped as rain started to pour; Tracy quickly legged it back to the barn and in through the hole in the side. Harlan and Cletus came out with Leon and approached the barn.

"Ah, damn weather, did you patch up that hole in the barn roof, Cletus?" said Harlan.

"No, sorry, Pa, I forgot," said Cletus.

"Well, for your sake, you better hope our guests don't die of hyperthermia," said Harlan as he opened the barn door and threw Leon inside. He was as battered and bruised as Jimmy was.

Everyone was there, including Tracy. The doors were about to close when Cletus noticed something.

"Wait, why are you wet?" asked Cletus while pointing at Tracy, who was partially soaked.

"Why do you think? She was standing underneath that hole in the roof and got soaked. Didn't it occur to you to fix it?!" said Cassie.

"Now don't get snippy with me, missy; I meant to fix that hole, I...I just forgot, I'm only human," said Cletus.

"Not even close," said Jimmy.

"What did you say to me, boy?!" said Cletus.

"Come on, Cletus, I'm getting soaked now!" said Harlan as Cletus left the barn and locked the doors.

Everyone sighed with relief.

"Did you get what we need?" asked Cassie as Tracy smiled and showed the glass.

"It may not look like much, but it'll get us out of here," said Tracy.

"Well, I really hope it was worth it; I just got my ass handed to me by those damn hillbillies," said Leon.

"Trust me, you get used to it," said Jimmy.

"You know I did this for you, Tracy, but there are some lines that shouldn't be crossed," said Leon as Tracy suddenly walked over and kissed him.

"Thank you, Leon" said Tracy.

"Uh, no...no problem," said Leon, slightly bemused.

"Oh, Jimmy, this is for you," said Tracy as she handed the knife to Jimmy.

"What's this, a fruit cutter? I asked for a knife," said Jimmy.

"What do you want, the knife used by Norman Bates in Psycho? Take what you can get; you can still kill someone with that," said Tracy as Jimmy sighed.

"Okay, everyone, just a little longer, then….we're leaving this place, all of us," said Tracy.

For the most part, everything was going to plan, but even the best-laid plans can go wrong.

Milford Sheriff's Department, Afternoon 1:00 pm

Agent Morgan was still waiting on some background information before questioning Joey. But Jim wasn't willing to wait until Francis had finished threatening and coercing him; he had to talk to Joey and find out what he knew and why he was being set up.

Sheriff Hanson arranged for Min to unlock the back door into the lockup while he kept Francis distracted. Min was talking to Joey while waiting for Jim.

"How is it in there?" asked Min.

"Well, I did always wish I could find out what it was like," said Joey with a small laugh; Min laughed, too.

"How's my case looking?" asked Joey.

"We're all working our hardest, we haven't given up," said Min.

"Glad to hear it," said Joey.

"You know, this should really be the moment where the story's main character kisses the girl through the bars," said Joey as Min chuckled.

"The hero gets the girl, right? And here I wasn't sure if you liked me," said Min.

"Of course, I like you, Min, I always have" said Joey.

"Then why didn't you say anything?" asked Min.

"I don't know, because I'm stupid?" said Joey.

Min and Joey then kissed each other through the bars. It was at that moment Jim came in the back door, and he couldn't help but smile at what he was seeing.

Min and Joey stopped kissing as they both stared at each other.

"Our movie moment" said Joey.

"Our movie moment," said Min.

Jim coughed.

"I'd better go, Joey, but don't worry, we won't leave you in here," said Min.

"I know," said Joey as Min blew a kiss and left.

"And I thought there were rules about canoodling in the lockup area," said Jim.

"Shut up," said Joey with a laugh.

"So, Min said you needed to talk to me," said Joey.

"Yeah, I wanted to conduct my own interview before Francis does," said Jim.

"Joey, can you think of any reason why Frank Boles would set you up or why he'd be doing this in the first place?" asked Jim.

"I've been wracking my brains since I was put in here, and nothing is coming up. I just don't get it; we've been friends since high school, we both had the same interests: to help people. I don't know why he'd turn like this," said Joey.

"And as for setting me up, well, I know we've had rusty communications with each other, but I don't recall doing anything that could warrant this," said Joey.

"It's alright, Joey, we'll figure this out. We're looking into Frank Boles' background, so we're bound to find something," said Jim.

"I'm glad you're on the case," said Joey.

"Jim, I hope you don't mind, but there's something I've been wanting to ask you; it's personal, though," said Joey.

"It's okay, Joey; you know you can speak your mind around me. What is it?" said Jim.

"Why do you hate Francis Morgan so much?" asked Joey.

Jim was quiet for a moment before he answered.

"Five and a half years ago, back when I was still in the FBI, there was this woman; her name was Matilda Sandra. She was beautiful, intelligent, sophisticated, strong, an incredible woman," said Jim.

"We were friends and partners the first couple of years after we met, but I fell in love with her. I found she and I had similar interests, likes and dislikes, and the biggest one of all was that she one day wanted to have a family, the same thing I've wanted for a long time," said Jim.

"Well, the FBI regulations frown upon fraternisation with co-workers, so Matilda and I found ways to meet in secret," said Jim.

"Any canoodling?" asked Joey with a smile.

"Lots of canoodling", said Jim, who smiled back.

"So, after about a year of sneaking around, we both decided that the only way we'd get the family we wanted was to quit the FBI and elope," said Jim.

"Something happened, didn't it?" said Joey.

"Yeah....Francis Morgan came onto the scene; he said he was working a big case and needed some backup. He was trying to bring down Alexi Sorkalov, one of the biggest dealers in DC, and had control over an entire half of the drug trade in the city," said Jim.

"Francis wanted Matilda to go undercover, posing as a client to set up a meeting and draw him out. I objected, of course, not only did Matilda not have enough experience in the undercover field, but according to Francis, the intelligence they had was shoddy at best, no ideas on the numbers, guns or the potential danger," said Jim.

"But Matilda pulled me to the side and said it was just one job. If we did take this guy down, it could be the pinnacle of our careers, finishing on a high note before we leave, so I agreed with her," said Jim.

"The next couple of weeks were quite tense, but Matilda had been able to infiltrate Alxei's organisation as a client and set up a meeting. She kept her cool and tried to stay in character," said Jim.

"Then, in the days leading up to the meeting, Matilda began expressing concerns that Alexi knew more than he was letting on, that her cover might not be intact. I went to Francis and told him to pull her out, but he said we were too close to the meeting; if we pulled out now, Alexi would know we were onto him, and he'd go to ground," said Jim.

"I begged him to see reason, but I let him talk me into thinking everything would be fine," said Jim.

"The day of the meeting arrived; it was in this big warehouse; we had all the exits covered, SWAT and other agents were standing by to burst in, and Francis and I were in contact with Matilda. But something went wrong….Matilda suddenly screamed into her earpiece that Alexi knew, and she was compromised; then there was a gunshot," said Jim.

"I called the calvary to raid the place; shots were fired on both sides; I frantically searched for Matilda. Then I found her….Alexi had shot her and left her to bleed out….I told her to hang on, but the paramedics weren't fast enough….she died in my arms," said Jim with tears in his eyes.

"Jim, I'm so sorry," said Joey.

"You know, I blamed myself for not being fast enough to save her. But then….my thoughts turned to Francis, and I realised it was him I should be blaming. He knew that Matilda wasn't ready for a job like that; he knew it was high risk, sending her into the lion's den with minimal intelligence. He put her life at risk, and he got her killed," said Jim.

"That's why I left the FBI; I couldn't stay there any longer; it was too painful. And I couldn't go on seeing Francis without wanting to kill him," said Jim.

"I'm so sorry you went through that, buddy; it's a horrible thing. You know, I actually know what it's like to lose someone," said Joey.

"You do?" asked Jim.

"My dad, he wasn't a good man; he didn't care about following the law or helping people; if there was money to be had, he'd take it. He was a criminal, or "triggerman" is the term; he worked for any crime boss that would sign him up; it didn't matter if he was killing people or selling them something", said Joey.

"David Brandon, my father, the biggest criminal in America and a disgrace to the family name", said Joey.

"I'm sorry, Joey," said Jim.

"It's okay; I got over it ages ago. I don't know what's become of him, whether he's alive or dead and quite frankly, I don't care," said Joey.

"So you see, we both lost someone we loved, and it affected us. But we both still turned out okay," said Joey.

"Losing someone you love can change you in many ways, and you never know it's happened until it does," said Jim.

Joey suddenly had a thought.

"Lindsay," said Joey.

"What?" asked Jim.

"Oh my god, Lindsay, why didn't it come up?" said Joey.

"Joey, you're not making any sense, who's Lindsay?" said Jim.

"Lindsay was a nine-year-old girl who lived in Milford. She was out on the back roads in Pike County when she was killed in a hit and run," said Joey.

"Well, that's really tragic, Joey, but how does that help us?" said Jim.

"Jim, Lindsay was Frank Boles's daughter," said Joey.

"It really hurt him what happened to her, I can't believe I didn't think of this. Oh, and guess what, the driver of the car who ran into her….was a teenager, and he was drunk off his skull," said Joey.

"I remember he told me the story; I've forgotten some of it because it was a few years ago we ran into each other by chance in the city. But I remember, the guy got away with it, he was let off on a technicality, and Frank was fuming; not only had he lost his daughter, but he'd also been robbed of her justice," said Joey.

"That might actually make sense; it would give a rough explanation as to why he's targeting teens. Maybe he looks out for any who are drinking and driving or just breaking the speed limit," said Jim.

"Well, the back roads are usually empty, save the occasional vehicle, but most people see it as a race track when it's clear," said Joey.

"A misguided attempt to avenge his daughter, it's all we have to go on," said Jim.

"Thanks, Joey, we'll get you out soon," said Jim as he headed for the main area.

"Wrong way!" said Joey.

"My bad," said Jim as he turned around and headed out the back exit.

Jim's House, Afternoon 2:05 pm

Jim returned to his house an hour later after he'd informed the Sheriff and Min about what Joey had told him. Once they had something, they were to convene at his house with their findings.

Jim looked out his window and saw the Sheriff and Min approaching; Violet and Eileen were also with them. He had very crudely put his door back up after Francis had kicked it right off the hinges; it wasn't fastened, though, which became moot after Sheriff Hanson reached out and knocked.

"Oh wait, Sheriff, the door's a bit-" the door fell in before he could finish.

"Loose", then he did.

"Sorry, my bad," said Sheriff Hanson.

"Come on in, everyone," said Jim as they all came into the living room and sat wherever they could find seats.

"So, do we have anything?" asked Jim.

"We certainly do. Your friend Dylan and I have been working hard on Frank Boles," said Sheriff Hanson as he showed his phone. Dylan was on a video call.

"Hey buddy, looking no worse for wear, I see," said Dylan.

"Thanks, so what do we have?" said Jim.

"Well, the Sheriff was checking Frank Boles's background while I was looking up the court case about his daughter, Lindsay," said Dylan.

"I didn't turn up much, sadly. Frank Boles joined the county police nearly fifteen years ago; he was a career police officer with nothing criminal in his file until after the incident with Lindsay. He then started getting written up for being late, for roughing up suspects and being aggressive to his fellow officers. They finally demoted him to a patrol officer and stuck him on one of the back roads in Pike County; that was the only interesting bit," said Sheriff Hanson.

"Okay, Dylan, what did you find?" asked Jim.

"Well, I looked up the court details, and I can honestly see why Frank was so pissed. The guy who ran into his daughter, his name was Micheal Reece, 18 years old, and he'd actually been out celebrating his first car with his friends, hence why he was drunk behind the wheel," said Dylan.

"When he was brought to trial, he and I quote, "Wouldn't stop crying on the stand." he was snivelling and said he didn't mean to hit Lindsay, that he tried to stop. Anyway, what really threw the case was the defence lawyer his parents hired; it says he got a lot of the evidence dismissed as theorised, and when nothing more concrete could be produced, they let his client go," said Dylan.

"That was the technicality that drove Frank over the edge," said Jim.

"There's more. Min, tell him what you found out," said Sheriff Hanson.

"So, I called a friend of mine who works in the county archives, and a week or so after the trial, Frank Boles started coming in all the time. He would ask for files relating to unsolved hit-and-run cases; he was particularly interested in anywhere the main suspect got off on a technicality or lack of evidence," said Min.

"This is apparently what led to Frank being late to work so many times. Min's friend confirmed the times he was there and how long for" said Sheriff Hanson.

"So, is Frank trying to avenge his daughter or become the next Batman?" asked Jim.

"The Batman sounds about right; a lot happens on those roads, and there's only so much that can be done about it," said Sheriff Hanson.

"Batman doesn't kill, though," said Eileen.

"Correctly put Eileen. Now, while it's always a pleasure to see you both, what are you doing here?" said Jim.

"Oh, we have some information. We had a call at the radio station from somebody who used to work with Frank and knew about his daughter's case. He said that there was another cop who was close to Frank and spoke to him a lot," said Violet.

"Do we have a name?" asked Jim.

"Yeah, we do," said Violet with some sadness in her voice.

"What's wrong?" asked Jim.

"Please don't be mad, Uncle Reg" said Violet.

"Why would I be mad, Violet?" asked Sheriff Hanson.

"The name of the cop....is Marlon Hanson," said Violet.

Shocked faces went around the room, except for Jim.

"Wait, Hanson, but Sheriff, doesn't that mean...." Jim didn't finish; he was waiting for the Sheriff to answer.

"Marlon Hanson is my brother and Violet's father. We haven't seen or spoken to him in years, not since the incident," said Sheriff Hanson.

"What incident?" asked Jim.

"Eight years ago, my mother and father were in a car crash out on the back roads. Dad survived; Mom didn't," said Violet.

"I'm very sorry, Violet," said Jim.

"I remember that it happened when I'd just moved to Milford. The whole town was up in arms, openly accusing Marlon of murdering his wife," said Min.

"Why would they do that?" asked Jim.

"In the days leading up to the crash, people around town had seen Marlon arguing with Alison, his wife, and one of the neighbours swears he heard him threaten to kill her. Alison was loved and cherished by everyone, so when news spread about what happened, they connected the dots," said Sheriff Hanson.

"What did Marlon have to say about this?" asked Jim.

"He was telling everyone that they were out on the road, another car came out of nowhere and sideswiped him, then he lost control and crashed the car," said Violet.

"And let me guess, the driver of the other car was never found," said Jim.

"No, we searched, but the driver and the car were long gone," said Sheriff Hanson.

"Anyway, Marlon started neglecting Violet, doing too much overtime at work and leaving her alone for hours, sometimes days. I mean, Eileen was there, thank god for her, but you still need some type of adult around," said Sheriff Hanson.

"Then, one day, he went to work and never came back. So I assumed the role of looking after my niece," said Sheriff Hanson.

"And you've done a great job, Uncle Reg," said Violet as Sheriff Hanson smiled.

"Do you think they could be working together?" asked Eileen.

"I would say I'm surprised, but time can change a man, especially after a trauma like that," said Sheriff Hanson.

Jim was then coming to a conclusion in his head, but it wasn't a good one.

"So, we know everything we can about the kidnappers and why they might be doing this, but a thought occurs. We don't actually know how to find them or where they're keeping Tracy and the other teens, do we?" said Jim.

Everyone looked at each other.

"No, we don't," said Min.

"We can't, I don't know, try the GPS in their car, presuming they are using a cop car?" asked Jim.

"I tried that. I called the county police, and they said Frank and Marlon haven't been back to work in the last month. Their uniforms, guns and the department-issued car are all missing, and they've disabled the GPS," said Sheriff Hanson.

Jim looked like he was really stressed out; he even started laughing a bit.

"You know, this all feels like some sick game. No matter how hard we try, we're never any closer to the end, the big finish!" said Jim.

"Jim, calm down," said Sheriff Hanson.

"We've been at this for days now, and every day that passes, more time is lost finding Tracy and the other teens. I mean, for all we know, they could already be dead!" said Jim.

"Jim, you can't think like that," said Min.

"Can't I? I was supposed to look after her, Min. I was supposed to be the guardian angel, but I took my eyes off her for a minute, and then she was gone. What kind of guardian does that? She's gone because of me….I can't….I can't take this!" said Jim as he stormed out of the house.

"Jim, Jim!" said Sheriff Hanson, but Jim didn't respond; he walked out with tears in his eyes.

Everyone looked at each other; they knew that Jim was feeling the stress of the whole case. They needed something, anything to give an indication as to where Tracy and the others were. But will they find the answer, or will it come to them?"

Chapter 16
Even the Best Laid Plans

Somewhere in the Pike County Wilderness

Back at the homestead, Tracy and the others were getting ready to enact their escape plan, her distraction was ready.

"Will this really work?" asked Cassie.

"Jim showed me how to make it; just gotta make sure we cover our eyes," said Tracy.

Jimmy was holstering the knife Tracy had got for him.

"You're not really planning on using that, are you?" asked Tammy.

"Tracy has made it clear that I only use it when we're in danger, and when that time comes, I will use it," said Jimmy.

"Tracy, can I talk to you?" asked Leon as Cassie walked away from them.

"Look, I just....I wanted to say I'm sorry....for getting you into this situation," said Leon.

"Well, it wasn't...entirely your fault; you had no idea there was some psycho cop out there. But still, you could've been more careful," said Tracy.

"Yeah, I'll have to remember that," said Leon.

"And Tracy, in case we don't make it, we will make it", Tracy interrupted Leon.

"But if we don't, I just wanted to say…you really are the best girl I've ever met," said Leon.

"Well….maybe you're not exactly like the other guys I've dated," said Tracy.

Leon then kissed Tracy. The others looked and expected Tracy to push him away, but she didn't.

Leon stopped and looked at her.

"For luck," said Leon.

"For luck," said Tracy with a smile.

"Okay, everyone, it's time to ditch this place," said Tracy as she and everyone headed for the hole in the wall. Tracy went through first to make sure the coast was clear; it was dark outside as night had fallen.

She signalled that it was all clear. After that, Cassie came through, then Tammy, followed by Jimmy and Leon. Everyone remained crouched down.

"Okay, now we head into the woods and try to find a road, gas station, a town, anything; let's go", said Tracy as everyone started heading for the woods.

Suddenly, a bright light illuminated them, and a siren went off. They all looked back and found it was coming from the police car in front of the farmhouse. Frank and Marlon stood on either side of it.

"STOP RIGHT THERE!!" said Marlon through the loudspeaker.

"Shit!" said Jimmy.

"GET OVER HERE, NOW!!" said Marlon as the group gave each other worried looks; they knew they had no choice.

Tracy led the group to the front of the car; Harlan and Cletus soon joined, surrounding them from the right side.

"And where do you all think you're going? It's a bit late for a stroll in the woods," said Frank.

"There's no way you could've known we were about to escape; it's impossible!" said Tracy.

"Like you thought it'd be impossible for us to know you broke into our house and stole a bunch of our stuff. We ain't stupid, girl," said Cletus.

"It was a valiant attempt but a fruitless one," said Marlon.

"Every one of you is deducted a chance for your little escape attempt," said Harlan.

"Now get back into the barn quietly without any fuss, and if you behave, maybe we won't neglect your dinner for the night," said Harlan.

"Why?" asked Tracy.

"Why? Because I told you to!" said Harlan.

"Not you; I'm talking to the cops. Like you, you're Marlon, aren't you, Violet's father?" said Tracy; Marlon didn't answer.

"Why would you both do this? You're cops; why would you kidnap innocent people and torture them like this?!" asked Tracy.

"Innocent? You really think you're innocent? Innocent people don't drink and drive; they don't break the speed limit or disregard road safety laws. Innocent people don't run kids over because they don't give a crap about who they hurt on the way!" said Frank.

Tracy was struck by a thought.

"You're Frank Boles, aren't you?" asked Tracy.

"How the hell do you know my name?" asked Frank

"I remember seeing you on the news a few years ago. Your daughter Lindsay was killed in a hit and run, and you fought like hell to make the driver of the car pay, but they released him on a technicality," said Tracy.

"The driver was a teenager; that's why you've been doing this. You're trying to avenge your daughter," said Tracy.

"My daughter and the hundreds of others who are run over and left to bleed out on the side of the road. Because drivers don't care, because they're worried about going to jail or losing their precious cars instead of doing the right thing!" said Frank.

"That's why Marlon is here. His wife was killed when he got sideswiped, and not only did the driver not pay, no one even believed him," said Frank.

"We're not the bad guys, Tracy; we're not villains. We are the vigilantes, the angels of justice, and one way or another, we'll make them all pay!" said Frank.

Suddenly, Jimmy shoved Tammy forward, which caused Marlon to fire. He shot Tammy while Jimmy ran over to Frank, pulled out the knife, then grabbed Frank from behind and held the knife to his neck.

"Back off, back off. Drop your guns, or he dies!!" shouted Jimmy.

"You just sacrificed Tammy!!" said Cassie.

"It was necessary; I told you that I'm avenging Derek. Now, we're leaving this place; if anyone follows us, I'll slit his throat!" said Jimmy.

"Your actions are very noble, Jimmy, but you may not be as brave as you think," said Frank.

"Shut up, you don't know anything!" said Jimmy.

"Oh, I know a lot, like I knew this was coming. Surprise!" said Frank as he suddenly pulled his own knife and stabbed Jimmy's leg. As Jimmy let go, Frank ran to the side while shouting, "Now!" a gun was pulled, and Jimmy was shot in the head.

Cassie screamed, "JIMMY!!!".

Tracy looked to see who shot Jimmy, it wasn't the cops, and it wasn't the rednecks. It was Leon.

"What the hell, Leon, what have you done?!!" asked Tracy.

Leon just stood there with the gun in his hand; he didn't say anything.

"Oh my god, you're working for them, aren't you?!" said Tracy.

"Not as simple as that little lady. You see, Mr Thornberg here made a deal with us; he'd tell us when you kids were planning to escape and help us kill the ringleader, young Jimmy, over there, and in exchange, we'd let him go," said Harlan.

Tracy stared at Leon with a new sense of betrayal. Leon looked back, all mournful.

"I'm sorry, Tracy," said Leon.

"Fuck you, Leon!" said Tracy.

"We had an agreement; I can go now?" said Leon.

"Go before we change our minds", said Frank as Leon started running into the woods; Tracy just watched as he went into the trees.

Leon had only made it so far when he suddenly fell down a hole into a pit that was filled with spikes. His scream was heard briefly, then nothing.

The cops and rednecks started laughing.

"Sounds like he found our spike pit, Pa," said Cletus.

While they were still laughing, Tracy took out the glass, pulled off the lid and put the tablet in the lemon juice; it started to bubble, she then stuck the lid back on.

"Hey, hey, what are you doing?" asked Frank.

"A little something sour," said Tracy as she shook the glass and threw it to the ground without breaking it.

Tracy and Cassie ducked and covered their faces; the kidnappers all looked at the glass as if it was bubbling, and they laughed again.

"It's bubbling, Pa," said Cletus.

"Oh, I'm so scared, son," said Harlan.

"Oh, I don't know which is worse, teenagers acting brave or actually being real dumb-" Before Frank could finish, the glass cracked and shattered, spraying the lemon juice in a wave onto the kidnappers and right into their eyes. They all cried out in pain and confusion as they rubbed their eyes. Tracy lifted herself up; she grabbed Frank's knife and used it to slash a couple of tires on the cop car. She then ran over to Cassie, and the two of them started running into the woods as fast as they could.

"My eyes are burning, Pa!" shouted Cletus.

"Argh, they're getting away!" shouted Marlon.

"No, they're not; get after them!" shouted Frank as he ran into the car and rolled off the hood.

Cletus grabbed hold of Harlan.

"I got one of them, Pa!" shouted Cletus.

"That's me, idiot boy!" shouted Harlan as he threw Cletus off.

Tracy and Cassie were running through the woods, trying to find the most stable pieces of ground that didn't require them to climb rocks or jump rivers. They just kept going and tried not to look back.

The kidnappers started to regain their eyesight by using some bottled water from the car to spray their eyes; they pulled themselves together and chased after the girls. The footprints in the mud were a dead giveaway as to the direction they'd gone.

As Tracy and Cassie had made some distance, Cassie suddenly tripped on a sticking-out root she didn't see and fell, accidentally pulling Tracy down as she dropped the knife, and it went into a bush.

"Cassie, are you okay?!" asked Tracy.

"I tripped....my ankle," said Cassie.

Tracy could hear voices behind them and saw lights in the distance.

"Come on, I'll help you!" said Tracy as she offered Cassie her shoulder and lifted her up. The two of them started moving again, but much slower now.

"Where's the knife?" asked Cassie.

"I dropped it. Come on!" said Tracy.

The kidnappers were getting closer, especially the rednecks. Like what was said before, they knew their way around the woods.

Tracy finally stopped as Cassie wasn't able to keep up her footing; they took cover behind a tree as the voices drew closer.

"Tracy, I can't run....my ankle is hurting...." said Cassie.

Tracy had to think fast.

"Just leave me, Tracy, just go!" said Cassie.

"No way, I've lost enough friends today; I'm not losing another!" said Tracy.

"But they're going to catch us!" said Cassie.

"No....they're going to catch me," said Tracy.

"Cassie, I'm going to distract them. When I do, you go as fast as you can; don't stop and don't look back!" said Tracy.

"But Tracy, they'll kill you!" said Cassie.

"Maybe, maybe not, but one of us needs to make it back to Milford. You have a good memory, Cassie; tell them these numbers, now focus," said Tracy as she told Cassie the map reference.

"Got it," said Cassie.

"Good, one more thing. If you see Jim, give him a message from me," said Tracy as she got up.

"Tell him, I really hope he finds me," said Tracy as she ran back into the woods. Cassie got up slowly and started limping the other way.

Harlan and Cletus came into a small clearing and saw Cassie in the distance; Harlan aimed his shotgun.

"Like shooting a turkey in a barrel," said Harlan as he went to pull the trigger.

Suddenly, Tracy appeared, kicking Cletus to the ground and hitting Harlan in the face with a small rock she'd found. Cletus got up and went for Tracy, who kicked him off balance then punched him in the face.

Cletus cried, "She hit me, Pa!".

Harlan got up and went for his gun, but Tracy knocked it from his hands, kicked him against the tree and punched him to the ground. Cletus tried to get up again, but Tracy threw the rock to knock him down again.

Tracy then heard a click behind her; she turned to see Frank standing there, holding his gun at her. Deep down, Tracy was terrified, but she didn't show it. As she stared Frank down, she knew what was coming; Frank pulled the trigger.

Cassie was nearing a road when she heard the shot echo through the trees. With tears rolling down her face, she came out onto the road and immediately saw a car coming towards her; the couple inside weren't looking until the wife cried out, "IN THE ROAD!!". The husband slammed on the brakes as Cassie ducked down with her hands out in front of her.

Shaw's Bar, Evening 10:30 pm

Jim was sitting at the end of the bar in Shaw's, gulping down the last bit of whiskey in his glass; he even had a full bottle next to him. The bar was mostly empty; everyone except Shaw had gone home. Sheriff Hanson and Min walked in.

"Where is he?" asked Sheriff Hanson.

"Other end of the bar" said Shaw.

"How much has he had?" asked Min.

"Just the one glass. He asked me to leave him the bottle, but I haven't seen him pour another," said Shaw.

"Probably for the best, thanks, Shaw", said Sheriff Hanson as he and Min went over and sat either side of Jim.

"We've been looking for you. Started to wonder if you'd gone rogue," said Sheriff Hanson.

"I went for a walk on the outskirts of town; I just needed to be alone for a bit, needed to think," said Jim.

"Jim, Tracy getting taken wasn't your fault," said Min.

"Can you swear to it....didn't think so?" said Jim.

"You know, I've been thinking a lot about family; it's something that I've wanted my whole life, to be a father of a son or a daughter. I had my shot....and it was taken away from me. For a while, I thought it was fate telling me that it wasn't meant to be," said Jim.

"When I saved Tracy from that photographer, and then her dad up and left, I saw her as someone who needed care and guidance, a guardian angel. And in the back of my mind, it felt like I'd been given a second chance. It didn't matter to me that we aren't blood-related" said Jim.

"And now she's gone too, and some part of me thinks that it was actually a cruel joke from fate, showing me that having a family really isn't on the itinerary. I failed her, Reginald....I failed Tracy, Derek, Mr Johnson, and I've even failed Joey. People always seem to get hurt when I'm around...I'm useless," said Jim.

"Alright, Jim, that's enough! I may let you do certain things your way, but I will not sit here and listen to you degrade yourself!" said Sheriff Hanson.

"Jim, you're one of the best things that happened to this town. When you first arrived, you helped to solve a murder case that, if left to us, would have seen an innocent man charged for a crime he didn't commit. And by the time we'd figured it out, it would have been too late," said Sheriff Hanson.

"You kept at it, and you solved the case. Everyone knew the kind of man Hicks Paxton was, they were ready to put the rope around his neck, but you saved him," said Sheriff Hanson.

"And despite not wanting this job in the first place, when people started coming to you with their problems, you didn't turn them away. Whether it was lost dogs, missing wallets, runaway pickup trucks or even kids skipping out on curfew, you were always there, trying your damnedest to help," said Sheriff Hanson.

"Now, I've looked after this town for a number of years, but there is always something that my deputies and I can't do, either because it sounds frivolous or because we don't have enough to go on. That's where you come in, Jim; you get between the lines, you go where we can't, and you find what we miss. That takes both a skilled person and someone who's determined to help people," said Sheriff Hanson.

"You didn't fail Derek or Mr Johnson. The poor kid was already dead; only those seers from Minority Report could've saved him," said Min.

"And you tried your best to help Mr Johnson; if Francis hadn't come in, he'd still be here. But that's on him, not you," said Min.

"We all know how much you care about Tracy, the things you've done for her in the past, the support you've given. You know to us, you're way more a father to her than an uncle, and she knows it too," said Sheriff Hanson.

"She needs you, Jim, Milford needs you....we need you, now more than ever," said Min.

"Milford needs a hero, Jim, and we think that could be you. You're more than just this town's first private investigator," said Sheriff Hanson as Jim put his glass down.

"Milford doesn't need a hero, Sheriff....it needs us," said Jim as he, Sheriff Hanson and Min all smiled.

"Come on, Mr PI, let's go to work!" said Sheriff Hanson as they all got up to leave. But the door opened up and revealed an unwelcome sight.

"There you are!" said Francis, who'd arrived with his agents.

"Goddamn it!" said Sheriff Hanson.

"I thought I might find you little hens here, clucking away to each other," said Francis as he and his agents approached them.

"This isn't the time, Francis," said Jim.

"Oh no, it is very much the time. I thought we had an understanding, Jim. Now I hear that you've been investigating behind my back, you've withheld information from me, and you've undermined my authority!" said Francis.

"Francis, just take the hint and leave!" said Jim.

"Oh no, you're not giving the orders here, I am. I told you that if you did anything to impede, interfere, disrupt or hampen my investigation, I'd regin you all in. Well, I've had enough; I'm putting dog collars on everyone and throwing them all into kennels!" said Francis.

"If that's all, then we're done here," said Jim as he tried to push past Francis, who grabbed his shoulder.

"We're not done!" said Francis as Jim suddenly turned and punched him in the face; the two of them started fighting.

Lincoln and Fitzgerald tried to reach for their guns, but Sheriff Hanson and Min jumped into action and fought with each of them, too.

Min elbowed Fitzgerald in the stomach, then hit him in the face; he regained his composure and tried to swing for Min, who dodged it, then karate kicked him in the face, knocking him down.

Sheriff Hanson grabbed Lincoln and knocked the gun from his hand; Lincoln swung for the Sheriff, who dodged him, then blocked his next attack and threw the man over his shoulder.

Jim and Francis were going at each other pretty hard; it seemed they both had a lot of anger. Min wanted to join in, but Sheriff Hanson stopped her.

"No, this is their fight," said Sheriff Hanson.

Jim punched Francis in the face, who punched him back and knocked him into a table. He went to punch again, but Jim grabbed his fist and delivered an uppercut that sent Francis smashing down onto one of the tables.

The agents were dazed and slightly bruised; Jim grabbed Francis on the ground and held him up.

"Now, I really hope you're conscious, Francis because I need you to listen to me very carefully," said Jim; Francis just groaned.

"This investigation is ours now. It should have been ours in the first place if you hadn't come along and thrown a wrench into the works!" said Jim.

"Our people are out there somewhere, and we're going to find them. Now I have half a mind to knock you out and ship you and your henchmen back to DC....but I'm not going to do that," said Jim.

"Instead, when you wake up, you'll have a choice. You can either flee back to Washington with your tails between your legs, or you can work with us to find the kidnappers and save our people. It's your decision, teamwork or tails," said Jim as he let Francis go.

Jim then went over to Mr Shaw and opened his wallet.

"When these men wake up, give each of them a drink, put it on my tab. And this should cover the table," said Jim as he put some money on the bar and walked away.

"Um, thanks, Jim," said Mr Shaw. Jim left the bar.

"I've never seen that side of Jim before; I don't know whether to be scared or attracted," said Min.

"Don't let Joey hear you say that; he might get jealous", said Sheriff Hanson as he and Min ran to catch up with Jim.

Mr Shaw just looked at the unconscious agents and thought to himself; this was the most fun night he'd ever had.

Jim's House: The next morning at 10:03 am

Sheriff Hanson and Min returned with Jim to his house; they started going over everything they'd found, looking for anything suspicious, hidden facts, undocumented information, anything to give an idea where the teens were. But sadly, they found nothing.

Jim retired to his bed during the night while the Sheriff and Min kept at it, but the both of them ended up falling asleep, too. Sheriff Hanson had his head down on the kitchen table, and Min was curled up on the couch.

Jim was sound asleep until his phone rang and woke him up. It was next to the bed, so he answered it.

"Hello?" said Jim tiredly.

"Jim, hey, it's Dom," said Jim.

"Hey Dom, what's happening?" said Jim.

"Sorry to wake you. I've been trying to reach the Sheriff, but he's not answering his radio," said Dom.

"Oh, it's okay; he's fast asleep on the table downstairs," said Jim.

"Oh, I see. Well, wake him up and then get down to the clinic fast," said Dom.

"What's the hurry?" asked Jim.

"It's Cassie Meadows, Jim; she was brought in early this morning. She's alive!" said Dom as Jim snapped out of his tiredness and went to wake the Sheriff and Min.

238

Chapter 17
In Plain Sight

Milford Clinic, Morning 10:15 am

Jim, Sheriff Hanson and Min raced over to the clinic as fast as they could. They came in the entrance and were greeted by Doctor Mcallister and Dom in the lobby.

"Doc, we heard Cassie Meadows is here," said Sheriff Hanson.

"Yes, she is, Sheriff, she's under observation at the moment," said Doctor Mcallister.

"Where did she come from? Is she okay?" asked Jim.

"Well, basically, she's been through hell, Jim. She has cuts and bruises to multiple areas of her body, and she's showing signs of dehydration and low blood sugar; she's also more than likely traumatised by the whole event," said Doctor Mcallister.

"As for how she got here, that couple sitting over there found her. They were apparently driving quite far into Pike County, heading for the next town to visit their son. They nearly ran into the poor girl. She was shaking and asked to be taken straight to Milford, so they did, as quickly as they could," said Doctor Mcallister.

"Min, interview the couple, find out what they remember", said Sheriff Hanson as Min went to carry out the interview.

"Dom, I want you to head back to the station to find out if Karen and Eric have those phone transcripts yet", said Sheriff Hanson as Dom nodded and left the clinic.

"Can we see Cassie?" asked Jim.

"I wouldn't advise that, Jim. We've done what we can to patch her up, but like I said, she's been through a lot and likely needs a lot of therapy and medical care," said Doctor Mcallister.

"Doc, Cassie is the one key lead. We have to locate Tracy and the missing teens; we have to take this chance," said Sheriff Hanson.

"We'll be gentle with her, Doc; you have our word," said Jim.

Doctor Mcallister still wasn't sure.

"Give me a moment," said Doctor Mcallister as he walked away.

"You okay?" asked Sheriff Hanson.

"A little nervous, worrying about hearing some answers that…I don't want to hear," said Jim.

Before Sheriff Hanson could say anything else, the doors to the clinic opened, and someone walked in.

"Jim," said Sheriff Hanson as they both turned round. It was Francis.

"Relax, I come in peace," said Francis as he stepped closer to them.

"I know I'm probably the last person you expected to see," said Francis.

"I thought you'd be on your way back to Washington," said Sheriff Hanson.

"The thought did cross my mind. I had quite a bit of time to think, actually, while sliding in and out of consciousness," said Francis.

"Jim, when I first arrived, I only had one purpose: to find Leon Thornberg; nothing else mattered. I tried to make it seem like I was the big boss, that I could do what I wanted because I had the FBI backing me. But now I realise that was wrong; a good agent always explores every possibility, and I did exactly the opposite," said Francis.

"You and I will always have a difference of opinion; we'll never agree on the same thing, and I know you'll never forgive me for Agent Sandra. But….I've made a choice, and if you have me, I'd like to see this case through," said Francis.

Jim and Sheriff Hanson looked at each other.

"You're right, Francis; I will never forgive you for Matilda or the things you've done to this town. But, as the case seems to be reaching its climax, we need all the help we can get," said Jim as Francis smiled a bit.

Doctor Mcallister came back.

"Cassie would very much like to speak with you guys," said Doctor Mcallister.

"Want to help us interview her?" Jim asked Francis.

"I'd be happy to", said Francis as he, Jim and the Sheriff followed the Doc to Cassie's room.

The three of them entered to see Cassie relaxing a bit in her bed, but her face lit up when she saw Jim.

"Jim!" said Cassie as he went over and hugged her.

"Hey, Cassie," said Jim.

"Sheriff!" said Cassie as she hugged him too.

"It's good to see you, Cassie," said Sheriff Hanson as they stopped hugging.

"Who's that?" asked Cassie.

"Special Agent Francis Morgan, FBI," said Francis as he extended his hand; Cassie reluctantly shook it.

"Right," said Cassie.

"So, Cassie, I realise you've been through hell, but if there's anything you can tell us about where you were being held, it would really help us", said Jim.

"Just take your time and tell us what you can, and feel free to leave out anything you don't want to remember," said Sheriff Hanson.

"The problem with that is I don't want to remember any of it," said Cassie as she took a deep breath.

"We were in Derek's car, me, him, Jimmy and Tammy, we were going to a club in the city. We….we stole some whiskey from Shaw's," said Cassie.

"I think, given the circumstances, we can excuse it," said Sheriff Hanson.

"We made it pretty far from town, but these cops pulled us over; we tried to bluff our way out, but they saw right through it. They handcuffed me, Tammy and Jimmy, and put us in the back of their car," said Cassie.

"But Derek....oh god....they handcuffed Derek, then one of the cops pulled a gun on him....Derek started running....and the cop shot him....then went over and shot him again to finish him off!" said Cassie, now with tears rolling down her face.

"We know about Derek, we found his body," said Jim as Cassie was trying to pull herself together.

"Where did the cops take you?" asked Sheriff Hanson.

"I don't really remember the journey. One minute we were in the cop car, then....we were waking up, chained in this barn," said Cassie.

"You were on a farm?" asked Sheriff Hanson.

"It was more of a homestead, I think," said Cassie.

"Was anyone else there?" asked Jim.

"Yeah, it wasn't just the cops; there's also these two rednecks, an older one and his son, in his twenties, I think. They would come into the barn, armed with shotguns and take each of us into this farmhouse across the way, then....they'd torture us," said Cassie.

"Me, Tracy and Tammy, they just cut us and shouted threats at us, but people like Jimmy and Leon, they actually got beaten up," said Cassie.

"Wait, Leon, as in Leon Thornberg, he was there?" asked Francis.

"Yeah, he arrived with Tracy about a day later; they said they were driving, and the same cops that got us ran them off the road", said Cassie.

"Tracy was definitely there too?" asked Jim.

"She's the reason I'm here," said Cassie.

"Did the rednecks feed you anything?" asked Sheriff Hanson.

"A little, not much," said Cassie.

"Okay, what happened next?" asked Jim.

"Tracy tried to help us plan an escape. She found a hole in the side of the barn said you'd taught her about observing an environment for weak spots to exploit," said Cassie.

"That sounds about right," said Jim.

"She snuck out and went into the farmhouse to get some things we'd need, planning a distraction" said Cassie.

"So what happened during the escape?" asked Jim.

"We got out of the barn and tried to run, but they caught us…. Tammy….oh god," said Cassie.

"What happened?" asked Jim.

"Jimmy….he pushed Tammy at one of the cops, and he shot her…..then Jimmy grabbed the cop who shot Derek and put a knife to his throat. Tracy got it for him; he really wanted to kill that cop for Derek," said Cassie.

"Did he?" asked Jim.

"No, he didn't, because that son of a bitch Leon shot Jimmy!" said Cassie.

"What?!" asked Francis.

"Leon made a deal with the kidnappers. He'd tell them about our escape, and they gave him a gun to kill Jimmy with. In exchange, they'd let him go," said Cassie.

"So what happened to Leon?" asked Francis.

"He started running into the woods, but he didn't get far before we heard him scream. Then the redneck boy said something about finding their spike pit; we connected the dots," said Cassie.

"I see," said Francis with a big sigh.

"So what happened next?" asked Jim.

"Tracy set off her distraction, a lemon bomb she said you taught her to make," said Cassie.

"Sounds about right, too," said Jim.

"It exploded and blinded the kidnappers temporarily. Tracy took the knife from one of the cops and slashed a couple of tires on their car, then we started running into the woods, a different direction than Leon went," said Cassie.

"The kidnappers regained their sight and started chasing us, we were quite far ahead, but those two rednecks warned us before that they knew the woods well," said Cassie.

"Did Tracy get away?" asked Jim.

"No…..during our run, I tripped on a rock or a branch, I don't know, I fell and twisted my ankle. Tracy helped me up, and we kept moving, but we were going slower, and the kidnappers were getting closer," said Cassie.

"Finally, Tracy said that she'd hold them off while I kept running. I didn't want to leave her, but she was adamant. So I ran, and I could hear her fighting them….but then….she…." Cassie was trying to stop herself from crying again.

"What happened to Tracy?" asked Jim with some worry.

"I don't know….there was a gunshot….and everything went quiet," said Cassie.

"Did you actually see her get shot?" asked Sheriff Hanson.

"No," said Cassie.

"They haven't killed her, Jim; they can't afford to. With all their charges gone, they'll need her alive to use as leverage," said Sheriff Hanson.

"I hope you're right," said Jim.

"Cassie, did you hear the names of the cops at all? Were they ever identified with them?" asked Sheriff Hanson.

"Yeah, one of them was Marlon, Violet's father; we haven't seen him in ages. The other one, Tracy, called him "Frank Boles". I think she said something about his daughter being killed in a hit and run, and Frank was saying something about "being the angels of justice"; that's all I remember from that", said Cassie.

"Cassie, do you remember anything about where you might have been? Can you show us where it is?" asked Francis.

"Sort of. Tracy took some basic readings off a map she found in the farmhouse. I still remember them, like I still remember the experience," said Cassie.

"Can you give them to us?" said Francis as he wiped out his notepad. Cassie told him the numbers, and he wrote them down.

"Thank you, Cassie, you've been a great help to us," said Francis.

"Wait, Jim, Tracy asked me to give you a message if I made it back to Milford," said Cassie.

"What's the message?" asked Jim.

"She wanted me to say, "I really hope you find me," said Cassie as Jim struggled to keep the tears back himself.

"Thank you, Cassie, and I promise I will find her," said Jim.

"We all will", said Sheriff Hanson.

Everyone then left the room to give Cassie some peace and mull over the information.

"I'll give these numbers to a friend of mine and ask him to triangulate an approximate location", said Francis as he quickly got on his phone.

"Well, he's certainly being more helpful; maybe you actually knocked some sense into him," said Sheriff Hanson.

"It did feel good to do that," said Jim.

"Sheriff!" suddenly said a voice as a female deputy came running up to them.

"Karen, what's wrong?" asked Sheriff Hanson.

"Me and Eric went through all the phone transcripts for this month; the calls with the unregistered number all came from Joey's phone," said Karen.

"Well, that doesn't help his case," said Jim.

"No, no, you don't understand. The calls were made with Joey's phone, but he wasn't the one making the calls," said Karen.

"Oh, of course. Use Joey's phone so it'll track back to him," said Sheriff Hanson.

"Did you find out who was making the calls?" asked Jim.

"We managed to decrypt who made the number and…well, you better see for yourself," said Karen as she handed the document to Jim; his eyes widened with shock.

"Oh no," said Jim.

Milford Radio Station: Morning 10:45 am

Violet had just finished the morning edition of her show, and she and Eileen were already chatting away with each other about various things. But the conversation was broken up by someone knocking at the door to the studio; Violet unlocked the door and opened it.

"Hey, Dom," said Violet.

"Hey Violet, can I come in?" said Dom.

"Sure," said Violet as she walked Dom in.

"You're a little late for the interviews; you'll have to." Violet stopped when she saw Dom lock the door.

"Why did you lock the door, Dom?" asked Violet.

"Just to give us some privacy," said Dom.

"Okay, Dom, you're freaking us out a little, maybe we should-" Eileen stopped and gasped as Dom pulled out his gun.

"Stay right here; that's a great idea, Eileen," said Dom.

"Dom, what the hell are you doing?!" asked Violet.

"Isn't it obvious? I'm taking you both hostage," said Dom.

"Yeah, I can see that; what I want to know is why?!" said Violet.

Eileen was next to the microphone and quietly switched it on.

Dom's veiled threats were suddenly being broadcast live over the radio; it was even heard in the clinic. That was enough for Sheriff Hanson and Jim to figure out where he was; they raced off as fast as they could.

"Let's be reasonable here, Violet. All you and Eileen have to do is remain still and wait for the Sheriff to arrive," said Dom.

Eileen was reaching for the microphone as Dom came closer.

"You're doing all this to get to my uncle?" asked Violet.

"It's for my survival and yours, Violet; what would Milford do without the Violet Show?" said Dom as Eileen suddenly swung the microphone and knocked the gun from Dom's hand, then hit him in the face with it.

Violet and Eileen ran for the door and unlocked it, but Eileen was grabbed by Dom as she tried to leave. Violet leapt onto Dom and tried to hold on; Dom threw Eileen to the floor and then did the same to Violet. He picked his gun back up.

"A nice attempt, Violet, but futile, to say the least," said Dom as he aimed his gun at her.

Eileen suddenly grabbed him from behind and tried to restrain him, but Dom broke free and backhanded her; Eileen fell to the floor as Dom was now aiming at her.

"I didn't want to do this, but I guess I'll just have to settle with one hostage instead!" said Dom.

"Eileen!" said Violet as Eileen closed her eyes.

Outside, multiple cars screeched up as the Sheriff, Jim, and the others arrived outside the radio station. They were about to head inside when they heard the shot.

"Oh god, NO!!" said Sheriff Hanson as he and everyone else ran inside.

They found the main studio; the glass had a hole, and there was fresh blood on the floor. Sheriff Hanson raced inside and saw Violet picking herself up.

"Violet, Violet, you okay?" asked Sheriff Hanson as he hugged her.

"I'm okay, Uncle Reg, I'm okay," said Violet.

"Sheriff," said Jim as he pointed to the corner of the room. Dom was sitting there with his hand bleeding.

"What happened, and where's Eileen?" asked Sheriff Hanson.

"Over there," said Violet with a smile.

Everyone looked and saw Eileen was fine, and the person hugging her was Old Man Wilson, her father, with a hunting rifle in his hand.

"Well, I'll be damned!" said Jim.

"I came by to bring Eileen some breakfast. I heard what sounded like a struggle, so I came in and....saw that bastard was about to shoot my daughter," said Wilson.

"You did great, Mr Wilson" said Sheriff Hanson.

Jim went over to Dom and kicked him to the ground as he tried to get up.

"It's been you this whole time, hasn't it? Using the traffic cameras to watch out for any teen-only cars leaving town, telling Officer Boles which ones to target, and making the calls with Joey's phone so that the transcripts would show it was him. You've been helping those kidnappers to snatch our people right off the road!" said Jim.

"I don't regret any of it; I'd do it all over again. We're not the bad guys, Jim; we're just doling out some justice of our own," said Dom.

"Vigilante justice isn't the way we do things!" said Sheriff Hanson.

"Speak for yourself, Sheriff; how many crimes have people gotten away with because it was outside our jurisdiction? How many kidnappings? How many carjackings? How many young sons like my boy?!" said Dom.

"Like Ben, my son, he came all the way down from the city to see me. And what happened? He was overtaken by a car of teenagers breaking the speed limit, and they ran him off the road!" said Dom.

"I trusted you, Sheriff; I followed you for years. But the one time I was really dependent on you to help me get justice, you told me you couldn't do anything, that it should be left to the county police. And guess what? They never found them!" said Dom.

"That's when you met Frank Boles, wasn't it?" asked Jim.

"I met Frank about a year ago at that support group for grieving families of hit-and-run victims. Frank and I got talking, and he told me about his daughter Linsday and how he was willing to do anything to avenge her, so the two of us came up with the plan," said Dom.

"We'd be the avenging angels for those who died on the back roads, we'd make them safer to drive, and nothing like jurisdiction was going to stop us!" said Dom.

"What about Marlon? Is he involved in this?" asked Sheriff Hanson.

"Oh yeah, he was more than happy to join us, especially given his own past experience," said Dom.

"His wife, Violet's mother, everyone blamed him for her death. But it wasn't his fault; they were run into, and no one believed him. Frank promised Marlon that they'd get justice the old-fashioned way," said Dom.

"What about these two rednecks?" asked Jim.

"They're just a couple of redneck psychopaths living in the woods; they were more than happy with the offer we made them," said Dom.

"What do they do to the captured teens?" asked Jim.

"Have fun, what else?" said Dom.

"Something else was bothering me. Was it really an accident that you told Mr Johnson his son was executed, or was it deliberately to make him lose it?" asked Jim.

"I had to stop Mr Johnson; his loud voice would have doomed us. What better way to get rid of him than for everyone to think he was crazy enough to kill himself or suicide by cop? Worked a treat," said Dom.

Francis had been on the phone during the conversation, talking with his friend about the map numbers.

"We have a possible location where the rednecks are based. The old Marston Homestead, deeper into Pike County," said Francis.

"Is that correct? Is that where they are?" Jim asked Dom.

"I'm not telling you. It's best to just sit back and let us do our work; it's all for the gre-ARGH!!!" Jim suddenly stomped on Dom's injured hand.

"Is that the location?!" said Jim as he pressed his foot down a bit harder; Dom was screaming in pain.

"Jim!" said Sheriff Hanson.

"Tell me!!" said Jim.

"Yes, it's there, okay, that's where they are, the old Marston Homestead. It's where the rednecks live; they have a barn where they keep the teens and a farmhouse they take them into and torture them; that's all I know!!" said Dom as Jim released the pressure.

Everyone was looking at Jim with some shock at what he'd done; he walked out of the room.

"Min, take Dom in", said Sheriff Hanson as he went after Jim; Min picked up Dom and cuffed him.

Jim was walking towards the exit when Sheriff Hanson stopped him.

"Jim!" said Sheriff Hanson.

"What?!" said Jim.

"That wasn't necessary!" said Sheriff Hanson.

"He's been right under our noses the entire time. If we'd only known sooner, we could have found Tracy and the others by now!" said Jim.

"I know Jim, and thanks to Cassie and Francis, we now know where to look. I know you want to find Tracy; we all do, but don't lose yourself in the process. Otherwise, the first words Tracy will say when she sees you is, "Who are you?" said Sheriff Hanson.

"She'd never say that to me," said Jim.

"Then don't give her a reason to", said Sheriff Hanson.

Jim walked out of the station; he needed to think.

Jim's House, Morning 11:05

Jim had returned to his home; he went inside and headed straight for his office upstairs. He walked inside and opened the desk drawer where he kept his gun, the one he hardly ever used. He lifted it out of the drawer and examined it. It'd been a long time since he'd ever had to shoot someone; now, it may be the only way to secure Tracy's safety. Jim then stared at the crime board he'd set up; it was Alexi Sorkalov he'd been trying to find, the man who killed Matilda Sandra.

For five years, he'd evaded the FBI and Law Enforcement, but Jim's thoughts turned to Matilda, things they talked about, things they planned, then the final words she said to him before she died. He never told anyone else about it; her last words before she died in his arms were, "Don't let this change you, be the man you know you are". As Jim's thoughts then turned to Tracy, he pulled out the clip, then put it back in and chambered the round. He holstered the gun, and before leaving the house, he said to himself, "Not again".

Milford Sheriff's Department, Afternoon 5:05

The next few hours were followed by meticulous planning between the Sheriff and the FBI. It might have made sense to set off as soon as possible, but the Sheriff felt that since the location would take them an hour and a half to reach by car, it'd be best to wait until nearly evening so that when they arrived, it would be dark, perfect for them to sneak onto the homestead without being seen. Jim wasn't too happy about the waiting, but time actually went by pretty fast.

Sheriff Hanson and Joey, who had been released from his cell, were loading their shotguns while Jim and Francis were loading their pistols.

"Sheriff, I don't see why it should be just the four of you going. Won't you need all the backup you can get?" said Min.

"Normally, yes, Min. But as two of the kidnappers are cops, if they see flashing lights and armed deputies coming, they'll run for the hills," said Sheriff Hanson.

"This way, going with a small number at the cover of night, we'll be able to sneak onto the property undetected and catch them off guard," said Sheriff Hanson.

"It's actually a solid plan, Min," said Joey.

"But Joey, it could be dangerous," said Min.

"We're deputies, Min, our job is dangerous," said Joey.

"But what if you get hurt?" asked Min.

"Relax, deputy, he's with us, we'll look after him," said Francis.

"Yeah, that makes me so much better," said Min.

Joey looked at Jim, who was lost in his thoughts.

"You okay, Jim?" asked Joey; Jim didn't respond.

"We're going to get her back, buddy," said Joey.

"I hope so," said Jim.

"Lincoln, Fitz, keep a close eye on our guest in the cells, don't approach him and don't question him until I get back, understood?" said Francis as both agents said, "Yes, sir".

"Okay, let's roll out", said Sheriff Hanson as the four of them headed for the exit. Min followed, too.

As they reached the car, Min tugged on Joey's jacket.

"Please be careful, Joey, I don't want to lose you", said Min as Joey put the shotgun against the car, then kissed Min in a passionate movie way.

"What is this, a damn romcom?" said Francis.

"Shut up, it's sweet," said Sheriff Hanson.

Joey stopped kissing Min as she was quite bemused.

"You'll never lose me," said Joey as he winked at her and then got into the car with the others. The car drove off into the distance. Min watched them as they went.

Chapter 18
A Daring Rescue

Milford Sheriff's Department, Afternoon 5:35

Almost half an hour had passed since Jim and Sheriff Hanson left. The department was just carrying on as normal, and the two FBI agents were watching Dom in his cell. He was just staring at the floor, occasionally looking up at the agents.

"Are you two just going to watch me all night?" asked Dom.

"Orders from Agent Morgan, we can't let you out of our sight," said Fitzgerald.

"Yeah, follow your orders like the good boys you are," said Dom.

Fitzgerald tried to approach the cell, but Lincoln stopped him.

"You know what, this is ridiculous. Why are we just playing a staring contest with this guy? He's not even staring back!" said Fitzgerald.

"Agent Morgan said to keep him locked up until he gets back," said Lincoln.

"And what if he doesn't come back? What if he, the Sheriff and that PI all get killed because this guy knows something, and we didn't get that information from him?" asked Fitzgerald.

"We need to question him while we have the chance," said Fitzgerald.

"We're not to let him out of the cell, Fitz!" said Lincoln.

"I'm not saying we let him out; we can question him in the cell; that's not breaching orders," said Fitzgerald.

While they weren't looking, Dom removed a fake piece of skin from his arm that revealed a hidden shiv the size of a small nail file.

Outside the lockup and in the main area, Min was heading in their direction when she stopped to talk to Karen.

"Hey Karen, are those FBI guys still in the lockup?" asked Min.

"Yeah, they've been there the last half an hour, won't let Dom out of their sight," said Karen.

"They said I'm not even allowed to bring him food, and I said "Well, that's good, 'cause that traitorous pig can starve anyway". I mean, can you believe he would do this to us?!" said Karen.

"I would've said no before, but after seeing him in action, I believe I can," said Min.

Back in the lockup, Fitzgerald was opening the cell; Lincoln stepped up to him.

"What the hell are you doing?!" asked Lincoln.

"I told you, I'm going to question him; you can come if you want," said Fitzgerald as he opened the cell.

"But Agent Morgan said not to talk to him!" said Lincoln as he followed Fitzgerald into the cell.

"Look, there's two of us, and we're both armed; if he tries anything, he'll regret it, won't you?" said Fitzgerald.

Dom didn't respond to the last comment.

"Hey, you awake there?" said Fitzgerald.

Dom still kept staring at the floor.

"Hey, I'm talking to you!" said Fitzgerald as he stepped forward. Dom suddenly rose from his seat and stabbed him.

"NO!" cried Lincoln as he went for his gun, but Dom quickly stabbed him too.

Min faintly heard Lincoln's cry from the main area.

"What was that?" said Min as she and Karen headed towards the lockup.

Dom grabbed Lincoln's gun, exited the cell and went through the back door.

Min came in a few seconds later and found the carnage.

"Oh my god, Karen, get help!" said Min as she entered the cell; she knelt down next to Lincoln, who was still breathing.

"Lincoln, hang on, that'll hurt a bit," said Min as she helped Lincoln take his coat off and used it to try to staunch his wound.

"Just hold it here, as tight as you can!" said Min as Lincoln tried to hold on.

Karen came racing back in with Eric behind her.

"We're locking down the station!" said Karen.

"It may already be too late; check him", said Min as she pointed to Fitzgerald. Karen knelt down next to him.

"Lincoln, where's Dom?" asked Min.

"He….went out….the back….he's got…my gun," said Lincoln.

Min got up and looked at Karen, checking Fitzgerald's pulse.

"He's dead," said Karen.

"Okay, stay with Lincoln until the ambulance gets here; Eric, with me," said Min as she and Eric drew their guns and went out the back door.

They came to the parking area just in time to see one of their patrol cars driving off into the distance. Min then noticed a deputy on the ground; feeling his head, she and Eric ran over to him.

"Kevin, are you okay?!" asked Min as she and Eric helped him up.

"Ah…it was Dom, he pistol-whipped me on the head….I didn't even see him coming…he took one of the patrol cars," said Kevin.

"Okay, I'll go after him, Eric; you look after Kevin," said Min.

"Wait, Kevin, where's your radio?" asked Eric.

"Dom must have taken it," said Kevin.

"Why would he do that?" asked Eric.

The sudden realisation struck Min.

"Frank and Marlon....Dom's going to warn them about Jim and the Sheriff...they'll be walking into a trap!" said Min as she ran for the nearest car, used her keys to start it and reversed the car up to Eric.

"Eric, organise armed backup and a couple of ambulances; tell them to follow the route to the Marston Homestead in ten minutes!" said Min as she drove off as fast as she could.

She had to try and reach the others before it was too late.

The Marston Homestead, Evening 7:09 pm

Night had fallen as Jim, Joey, and Francis were approaching the Marston Homestead; they walked up the small roadway while crouched down with their guns at the ready. As they got closer, they found it was eerily quiet.

"Something doesn't feel right; they should have someone patrolling," said Francis.

"You disappointed?" asked Joey.

"I'm not, but no guard usually signifies a trap," said Francis.

"Well then, there's only one thing we can do," said Jim.

"And that is?" asked Joey.

"Spring the trap," said Jim as he led them towards the farmhouse.

As they drew closer to the front door, Marlon was hiding behind a tree not too far from them and taking aim.

"Like rats in a trap," said Marlon as he suddenly heard a click from a couple of metres behind him.

"Marlon," said Sheriff Hanson, he'd snuck around the side of the property.

"Reginald," said Marlon as he dropped his gun.

Jim and the others burst in through the front door without any trouble. They regrouped in the hallway.

"Okay, Joey, you secure downstairs; Francis and I will go up," said Jim as Joey nodded and went into the living room. Francis and Jim started to climb the creaky stairs.

"Shhh," said Jim.

"It's not my fault; it's these stairs", whispered Francis.

Back outside, Sheriff Hanson was keeping a close watch on Marlon.

"I suppose you must think I'm a monster," said Marlon.

"Among other things. You're a disgrace, Marlon; in all the years of us growing up, I never imagined you could have fallen this far. How could you do this to Violet?!" said Sheriff Hanson.

"Leave my daughter out of this!" said Marlon.

"She already knows you're involved, Marlon. How do you intend to explain all this away, the kidnapping, the murders? Tell me how!!" said Sheriff Hanson.

"I'm not the bad guy here, Reggie; I'm saving lives!" said Marlon.

"Saving lives is that what you call it?!" said Sheriff Hanson.

"Do you think I liked leaving everything behind, abandoning Violet? I had to leave, Reggie; the whole town thought I was a murderer; they wouldn't believe me when I told them I was sideswiped by a reckless driver. I couldn't save my wife, but I can save other people, and Violet will see me as a hero," said Marlon.

"She won't see you in anything except prison leathers. Enough's enough, Marlon, now put your hands-(BANG).

A shotgun suddenly fired behind Sheriff Hanson as he collapsed to the ground; Frank had fired the shot.

"Sorry, Sheriff, but the fun's only just started," said Frank as he aimed to fire again.

"No, he's mine!" said Marlon.

"Fine, he's all yours," said Frank as he ran towards the farmhouse.

Inside the house, Francis and Jim had reached the top of the stairs, and both split up to look around. Jim found the door to Cletus's room; he grabbed the door handle and slowly opened it. As he looked inside, he saw a sight that filled him with joy. Tracy was lying on the bed with straps around her hands, tying her to the bedposts. She had a plaster on the left side of her head; Frank hadn't killed her, only grazed her.

Tracy slowly opened her eyes as Jim quietly called for Francis to come over; he slowly did. Tracy saw Jim in the doorway, but she didn't react; that was because Harlan and Cletus were in the room, too, hiding and getting ready to ambush them.

Francis was about to walk in, but Jim stopped him. He knew the look of worry on Tracy's face; quietly, he mouthed, "Is anyone else in the room?". Tracy blinked once; that was the signal for yes. Jim nodded to Francis as he walked in. Seconds after, he ducked as Cletus swung his knife but hit the wall instead. Francis then came in but had the gun knocked from his hands by Harlan, who tried to aim his shotgun, but Francis grabbed it and struggled as it went off; luckily, no one was hit.

Joey was in the living room when he heard the commotion upstairs; he turned to head out when he saw Frank standing in the doorway.

"Hey buddy," said Frank as he fired a shot at Joey, who leapt behind the couch he was next to. Joey returned fired as Frank ducked behind his own couch; the room had two of them, and they started trading shots at each other.

Outside, Sheriff Hanson was still on the ground as Marlon approached him.

"It's a shame we saw you coming; it might have been better if it was a surprise", said Marlon as he turned the Sheriff onto his back, only for him to suddenly kick him in the knee and then in the face. Sheriff Hanson got up; he was okay.

"Double vested?" said Marlon.

"What else?" said Sheriff Hanson as Marlon charged him. The two of them engaged in combat as they both threw punches at each other. This was a brother-on-brother fight, and both had training through past experience.

Inside the house, Jim and Francis managed to gain the upper hand and knocked both Cletus and Harlan down. Francis kept watch while Jim went over to the bed and untied Tracy. As soon as she was free, she hugged him tightly, and Jim hugged her back.

"I knew you'd find me!" said Tracy through her tears.

"I'm sorry I took so long!" said Jim with his own tears.

"Are you okay?" asked Jim.

"Much better now that you're here," said Tracy.

The two of them stopped hugging; it was hard.

"Wait, Cassie, did Cassie make it?!" asked Tracy.

"Cassie's fine; she's at the clinic," said Jim.

"Oh, thank god!" said Tracy.

"Can we save the emotional reunion for when this place is secure?" said Francis.

"Who are you?" asked Tracy.

"Special Agent Francis Morgan, FBI at your service" said Francis.

"Come on, Tracy, let's go," said Jim as he led Tracy out of the room.

"Now, you boys keep still, and we won't have any trouble," said Francis.

"We won't have any trouble, but you will!" said Harlan as he suddenly kicked Francis in the shin and then in the face; Cletus leapt up and pinned Francis to the floor.

"I got him Pa!" said Cletus.

"That's my boy," said Harlan as he picked up his shotgun and left the room.

Jim and Tracy had just reached the stairs when Harlan emerged and fired a blast that just missed Tracy and hit the wall by the stairs.

"RUN!" cried Jim as they ran down the corridor towards the other end. He fired two shots from his pistol, but Harlan took cover as they missed. Jim and Tracy kept running as more blasts were fired at them. Tracy's shoulder charged the door to Harlan's room as they both went inside and closed the door.

Jim barricaded it with a cabinet that he pushed in front of the door; Harlan was then heard pounding on the other side.

"Jim, you're bleeding!" said Tracy as Jim saw some red on his sleeve.

"It's just a nick; I'll be fine," said Jim as Harlan kept pounding on the door.

Jim noticed there was a side door of sorts in the room; he quickly pulled it open and saw it was a wooden walkway that led to what looked like the garage. As Harlan suddenly fired a blast through the door and started destroying the cabinet, Jim pulled Tracy out as they headed across the walkway. They found another door that Jim was able to shoulder charge open just as Harlan burst into the room above them; he saw where they went and fired a shot that missed as they went into the garage.

Inside the living room, Joey ran out of shells as Frank had the same problem; he got up and fled out the room as Joey pulled his pistol.

"FRANK!!" shouted Joey as he followed him out of the room.

Upstairs, Francis was able to use some pepper spray he kept in his pocket to get Cletus off of him.

"Ah, my eyes, not again!" shouted Cletus as he quickly regained his composure and attacked Francis, who fought back with everything he had.

In the kitchen, Joey went inside, but he couldn't see Frank. As he looked about, it was that eerie quiet again. Just as Joey turned, he saw Frank too late. He charged him into a series of shelves on the wall, and they fell down as Joey hit them. Frank grabbed Joey as he tried to throw a punch, but it was deflected as Frank got hold of him and aimed his own pistol at Joey's head.

"Just close your eyes, Joey; it'll be over before you know it," said Frank.

"Let him go!" suddenly said Min, who was standing in the doorway to the kitchen, shotgun in hand.

"What the?" said Frank as Joey took his chance; he elbowed Frank in the stomach and broke free of his grip, throwing himself to the ground as he shouted, "MIN NOW!!".

As Frank regained his balance and aimed to shoot Joey, Min fired off a blast that just hit Frank's vest and knocked him back a bit. As he then aimed to fire at her, Min let off another blast closer to his chest; that was the killing blow as Frank fell to the ground dead.

Min collected herself and raced over to help Joey up; the two of them hugged each other.

"Min, boy am I glad to see you!" said Joey.

"It's a good thing I got here in time," said Min as they stopped hugging.

"Joey, Dom broke out of his cell. He killed one of the agents and injured the other; he was on his way here to warn everyone that you were coming!" said Min.

"Then we'd better find the others!" said Joey as he and Min headed out of the kitchen. Joey stopped and looked back at Frank.

"Sorry, buddy," said Joey.

"Come on, Joey!" said Min as Dom suddenly appeared and tackled her; Min's shotgun went off and fired a blast that Joey just managed to dodge as it went through the window in the kitchen. Dom tackled Min down the stairs to the basement, then kicked her inside and closed the door. Joey ran over to try and stop him, but it was too late, the door locked from the other side.

"DOM, DOM, LET HER GO; IF YOU HURT HER, I'LL MAKE YOU REGRET IT!!!" shouted Joey as he tried to open the door.

Inside the torture room, Dom looked at Min as she got up.

"You know something, Min, I never really liked you," said Dom as he cracked his knuckles.

"The feeling's mutual, Dom," said Min as she dropped into a karate fighting stance.

The two of them then charged each other, with Min displaying an amazing knowledge of karate, but Dom also had a surprising amount of fight training. Joey could hear the fighting inside as he kept trying to open the door.

Min and Dom kept going at each other, with Dom swinging some punches, only for Min to karate kick him down when he made his moves, but Dom also dodged a few kicks and used it to land some hits on Min.

Outside, Sheriff Hanson and Marlon were still throwing punches, as well as each other around. But Marlon then gained the upper hand when he used a kick move to knock Sheriff Hanson down. Then, he moved in and wrapped his hands around his throat; he started squeezing as the Sheriff struggled to breathe.

"It's nothing personal, brother; I'll make sure to send your regards to Violet!" said Marlon as he tightened his squeeze. Sheriff Hanson struggled to stay conscious as his breathing was lessening until….

"ARGH!!" Marlon screamed as he let go and fell to the side; Sheriff Hanson had been able to reach for his trusty penknife and stuck it into Marlon as hard as he could. It wasn't enough to kill him, but it wounded him enough that he couldn't fight anymore.

Breathing heavily, Sheriff Hanson got up and looked at his wounded brother.

"What are you waiting for….finish it….do away with me!" said Marlon.

"No," said Sheriff Hanson.

"Why, because you're the Sheriff?!" said Marlon.

"Because Violet would never forgive me, love or hate, you're still her father. Even the monster you've become," said Sheriff Hanson as he picked up his shotgun and started running towards the house.

Inside the garage, Jim and Tracy had set up a sizable barricade against the side door. But now the problem of how they would get out was realised as Harlan started banging on the door, trying to break it down.

"We have to go out the front," said Jim as he led Tracy to the garage door. He saw a button that looked like the open and close mechanism. He pressed the button, but nothing happened.

"Damn it!!" said Jim.

Sheriff Hanson made it into the house and found Joey pounding on the basement door; he ran over to him.

"Joey, what's happening?!" asked Sheriff Hanson.

"Min's locked inside, Dom's attacking her!" said Joey.

Sheriff Hanson knew there was no time to ask, so he started trying to help open the door.

In the garage, Jim and Tracy tried to lift up the garage door, but it was really heavy. Tracy then started to pound on the door and shouted, "Help!" loudly.

Sheriff Hanson and Joey heard her cry.

"That's coming from outside!" said Joey.

"You go to it, Joey; I'll keep on with this door!" said Sheriff Hanson as Joey ran outside.

He looked around and quickly found the garage door.

"Hey, is anyone there?!" shouted Joey.

"Joey, it's me and Tracy, we're trapped in here, the door won't open!" said Jim.

Harlan was getting more aggressive with his banging on the side door.

"Let's all try lifting it!" said Joey.

"It's too heavy!" said Tracy.

"We have to try!" said Joey as he grabbed the garage door; Jim and Tracy did the same on their side. They counted to three and pulled upwards as hard as they could; the garage door started moving, they were doing it.

"Tracy, if you see a space, get outside!" said Jim.

"No way, I'm not leaving you!" said Tracy as they kept pulling. Harlan was close to breaking in.

In the bedroom, Cletus kept swinging at Francis, who finally got the upper hand by tripping him up with a leg swipe and knocking him down; then, he moved in and quickly cuffed Cletus to the radiator.

"Ah, no fair, we never said about using cuffs!" said Cletus as he tried to break free.

Francis collected his gun and walked out of the room.

"Now stay, there's a good boy," said Francis as he left the room.

But Cletus revealed that he had a lockpick hidden in his shoe and started to undo the cuffs.

Inside the basement, Dom and Min were both still fighting each other. Dom charged Min, only for her to move and trip him up; he fell onto the table with a tray of knives scattered on the floor.

Min came in close and held Dom by his collar.

"You're under arrest, Dom," said Min.

"In your dreams!" said Dom as he grabbed one of the knives on the floor and swung it towards Min.

Sheriff Hanson heard Min scream from inside.

"That's it!" said Sheriff Hanson as he used his shotgun to blow out the hinges and kicked the door down. He went inside and was shocked at what he found.

Dom was on the floor, still alive, but with a knife in his stomach, and Min had a large cut on her arm; she'd used it to deflect the knife attack, then turned it back and stabbed Dom with it. Again, not enough to kill him, but he was down for the count.

Sheriff Hanson raced over to Min.

"Min, are you okay?" asked Sheriff Hanson as he pulled out one of his handkerchiefs and gave it to Min, who held it on her cut.

"I'm fine Sheriff, I'll be okay," said Min.

Francis then came into the basement, gun in hand.

"Is everyone alright?" asked Francis as he saw Dom.

Sheriff Hanson helped Min up; she could still walk.

"All good; where's Jim?" said Sheriff Hanson.

"I don't know," said Francis.

"Wait, the voices outside everyone!" said Sheriff Hanson as everyone hurried out.

Jim, Joey and Tracy kept their hands on the garage door as best they could; Harlan was about to break in.

Just as the garage door lifted out of their hands as the automatic hydraulics kicked in and the way was open, Harlan burst through the door and took aim at Jim. In the split second before he fired, Joey ran in front of Jim and took the blast; he fell to the ground.

"NO!!" Jim cried out as he raised his gun and shot Harlan four times; Harlan fell against the wall and slid down dead.

Tracy took off her coat, then knelt down next to Joey and held it over his wound; it didn't look good. Jim knelt down next to him, too.

"Oh god, Joey!" said Jim.

"Is....is it....bad?" asked Joey, unable to breath very well.

"Joey, just try to breathe, okay? Keep still," said Jim.

"Easy for.....you to say," said Joey.

"You know....I prayed for....for one day....being able to....to save your life...instead of you...saving mine all the time," said Joey.

"Well, you did save my life, Joey," said Jim.

"Yeah….but now…you owe me one," said Joey.

Sheriff Hanson, Min, and Francis came out to the front of the house.

"JOEY!!" said Min as she saw him on the ground and ran over, kneeling down and holding his hand.

"Min….you're okay," said Joey.

"Joey, what did you do?!" asked Min.

"Oh….you know me….just being the hero," said Joey.

"What happened….to Dom?" asked Joey.

"He's been dealt with," said Min.

"Goddamn it, it'll take backup ages to get here!" said Sheriff Hanson.

"They're already on the way; I checked before I arrived," said Min.

"Then I guess we just wait now," said Francis.

Cletus then emerged from the side door to the garage with a crossbow in his hands; he found Harlan lying dead against the wall.

"Pa?" said Cletus as he looked angrily towards the others; he aimed his crossbow and fired the bolt.

"Look out!" said Francis as he moved Sheriff Hanson out of the bolt's path.

Cletus then ran out the door and jumped the barrier on the stairs.

"You goddamn sons of bitches, you killed my Pa!" shouted Cletus as he ran into the woods.

"Damn it, I thought I'd cuffed him. We have to go after him, Jim, come on!" said Francis.

"I can't leave Joey!" said Jim.

"We'll stay with Joey, you go with Francis," said Min.

"But Jim" Joey interrupted Jim.

"If he escapes…he could find new friends….and start this up….all over again…then what we did tonight….will have been for nothing," said Joey.

"I'll be fine…..go, Jim," said Joey.

"He's right; go get him, Jim Gold," said Tracy.

Jim finally realised they were right; he chambered his gun and ran around the garage with Francis; they spotted the footprints in the mud on the other side and followed them into the woods.

Jim and Francis split up as they went into the woods, keeping their guns firmly in front of them and checking their surroundings. It was eerily quiet, but with the sounds of faint footsteps and twigs snapping, it wasn't just them.

The two of them jumped at certain points when Cletus started shouting and taunting them; his voice echoed all around them.

"Can you see me….where am I….am I here….come and find me!" Cletus shouted at them, but they couldn't tell which direction it came from.

Jim and Francis were both breathing heavily at this point; Cletus was crazy, that much they knew, but how far was he willing to go to.

"ARGH!" Francis suddenly cried out as a bolt came from nowhere and hit him in the chest; he gasped at the sight of it sticking out.

"I got him, I got that FBI guy, you see that Pa?!!" shouted Cletus.

Jim heard it and felt a sudden dread. He kept moving forward and seemed to be coming to a clearing, but as Jim rounded a corner by this tree, he ducked down.

An axe suddenly swung for him and hit the tree; it was Cletus; he'd led Jim to a spot where he and his Pa used to cut down trees, hence the axe. Jim aimed his gun, but it was knocked from his hands before he could fire.

Cletus swung the axe at Jim as he kept dodging it as best he could; he swung again but hit the tree instead. Jim got in a punch as Cletus kicked him away, freed the axe from the tree and went for him. Jim grabbed the axe, and the two of them struggled with it, both trying to break it free from the other.

But Cletus cheated and headbutted Jim, then hit him with the wooden handle of the axe. Jim fell to the ground, slightly dazed, as Cletus sat on top and started to strangle him with the axe. Jim tried to move it, but Cletus was surprisingly stronger.

"THIS IS FOR MY PA, ASSHOLE!!" cried Cletus as he tightened his grip and Jim was close to death.

Suddenly, a gun went off, and Cletus cried out as he was hit on his shoulder; he fell off Jim and dropped the axe. Jim regained his senses and looked up to see Francis holding his gun up as he fell against a tree and slid down, the bolt still in his chest.

Cletus looked and saw Jim's gun on the ground; Jim then saw Cletus's axe not too far from him. Both of them reacted as Cletus went for the gun; he grabbed it and turned just as Jim reached for the axe and threw it at Cletus with all his might. Cletus cried out as the axe hit him in the chest, and he fell to the ground.

"I'm….sorry….Pa," Cletus stopped breathing.

Jim got up and ran over to Francis, who was barely conscious after losing so much blood. He knelt down next to him.

"Francis, Francis!" said Jim.

Francis started to wake up slightly.

"Francis, just stay with me; help will be here soon," said Jim.

"No, don't….don't waste your time on me, Jim," said Francis.

"Come on, Francis, don't give up. We did it, we won!" said Jim.

"No, you won….and that's what everyone is going to know," said Francis.

"There's..something I need to tell you…about Matilda," said Francis.

"Francis….what happened to Matilda was a long time ago….and I've held onto the hate for you because you were the easiest to blame…and I shouldn't have", said Jim.

"No, no….you were right Jim….you know why….because I knew….I always knew," said Francis.

"What are you talking about?" asked Jim.

"I knew….the kind of man Alexi Sorkalov was….I knew the intelligence was next to nothing….and I knew Matilda wasn't ready for a job that big," said Francis.

"But I sent her anyway….straight into the lion's den….so that I could get that promotion I always wanted" said Francis.

"I needed a big win….to impress the Director….I used you….and I used Matilda….to climb the ladder," said Francis.

"So you see….you were always right to hate me….I'm not a good person….I'm not a good man," said Francis.

"I'm….sorry….Jim….I'm….so…." Francis stopped breathing.

Jim checked his pulse; Francis was dead. Jim slowly got up from the ground and started to walk away; he was stunned by the confession he'd just heard and didn't know what to think. The man he'd hated the last five years had been responsible for Matilda's death all this time after denying it for so long. As Jim got a few metres away from Francis's body, he stopped and then looked back at him.

"I forgive you, Francis," said Jim as he continued to walk away. He never thought he'd ever say that to Francis but felt that it was time to move on from the past. He'd never forget Matilda, but he wouldn't be consumed with guilt any longer.

Jim came back to the farmhouse as the familiar flashing lights and siren sounds indicated that backup had arrived. Armed deputies and county police were entering the farmhouse and barn. A couple of ambulances were there, too. Jim caught sight of Min sitting in one of them as the doors closed, and it started to drive away.

Jim went over to Tracy, who ran over and hugged him tightly; tears were rolling down her face. Jim looked at Sheriff Hanson; he didn't look happy; in fact, he seemed to be close to tearing himself up. Jim asked about Joey; Sheriff Hanson looked at him and shook his head. Jim came to the realisation of what was happening, but he didn't know if they meant that Joey had died or if his condition was beyond critical. Soon enough, a new feeling of guilt was flooding Jim, and this time, if the worst happened, he'd never forgive himself.

Chapter 19
A Shocking Revelation

Three Months Later

The next three months were hard on everyone as they tried to come to terms with the horrifying experience that'd happened within the county. Jim exited his house with a bouquet of flowers in his hand; he climbed into his car, placing the flowers on the backseat, then started the car and drove into town. He shortly arrived outside Tracy's house, then stopped and honked his horn. Tracy came out a few seconds after; given what she went through, she'd cleaned up pretty well and looked healthy again. Tracy had her own bouquet of flowers; she climbed into the car and placed them on the back seat while saying "Hey" to Jim.

"You okay?" asked Jim.

"Yeah, I'm good," said Tracy.

"Okay then, let's go pick up Cassie," said Jim as he started driving away.

Jim then arrived outside Cassie's house and honked the horn. She came out with yet another bouquet of flowers, also looking healthier and cleaner than before. She climbed into the back of the car without squishing the flowers and placed hers on the pile.

"Hey," said Cassie.

"Hey," said Tracy and Jim.

"You ready?" asked Jim.

"Yeah, I'm ready," said Cassie.

"Me too," said Tracy.

Jim nodded and drove the car to the Milford Cemetery.

As they arrived and climbed out of the car with their bouquets, Jim noticed the crowd that was waiting for them halfway into the cemetery. The three of them walked over to the crowd.

Sheriff Hanson, Todd Hunter, Old Man Wilson, Eileen, Violet, Gomez, Miss Salazar, Shaw, Rose and Doctor Mcallister were all there, facing the grave.

Jim, Tracy and Cassie stopped in front of the grave and stared down at it.

"Do you think these will do?" asked Jim as the sound of a squeaking wheel was heard, and a wheelchair was pushed next to him.

"Yeah, I think they'll do," said Joey.

Joey had miraculously survived the shotgun wound and been confined to a wheelchair for the next few months until the doctors felt it was safe for him to walk again. Min had been by his side the entire time and was also the one pushing him in his wheelchair.

Jim smiled as he, Tracy and Cassie each placed their flowers on what turned out to be three graves in front of them. They belonged to the Johnson family: Derek, his father and his mother.

"May God grant this family the peace that they deserve?" said Jim.

A while passed as everyone had a little something to say about the Johnsons before they all left after it was done.

As everyone was walking away, Jim and Tracy were still by the graves.

"Are you coming?" asked Cassie.

"Yeah, I'll be with you in a moment," said Tracy as Cassie smiled and walked away.

"Are you coming for a drink?" asked Joey.

"Yeah, you two lovebirds, go on ahead; I'll catch up," said Jim as Min pushed Joey away.

Agent Lincoln also survived his injuries thanks to the surgical work of Doctor Mcallister. This, however, gave him the unpleasant job of having Francis and Fitzgerald's bodies shipped back to DC and explaining to the FBI what had happened. The Director stated that both of them would receive a proper funeral for their service to their county, and Lincoln was even offered a commendation for his involvement. They offered one to Jim as well, given his past FBI experience, but he turned it down.

Jimmy and Tammy had also been given proper funerals that everyone attended. Leon Thornberg's body was shipped home to his parents so they could arrange his funeral. Not that they were happy about the condition he'd been found in or the accusations that were levied against him. They threatened a more thorough investigation into the matter with more capable agents.

But not everything was all doom and gloom. Miss Salazar's kidney transplant was a success, and her health was improving by the day.

Despite not getting his nest egg back, Todd bought the story that he was the target of a random thief, and his friendship with Gomez remained intact. Based on a lie, but no one needs to tell him that.

To everyone's surprise, after the events of the kidnappings and Dom's betrayal, Todd and Old Man Wilson's hatred for each other actually decreased. They've now started talking to each other, small talk mostly, but they're able to get by without shouting or swearing at each other. Eileen's relationship with her dad also improved as a result of him saving her life.

Sheriff Hanson told Violet about what went down with her dad, Marlon, and given that he and Dom were the only ones to survive, they were facing the full brunt of the charges, kidnapping, assault, murder, abuse of authority and many more. Violet seemed content that it was over, but Marlon was already sending visiting requests to her; whether or not Violet will hear what her father has to say remains to be seen.

Doctor Mcallister delivered his diagnosis of Miss Kean to a doctor friend of his, working in a city hospital. After having more tests done, they confirmed Miss Kean's dementia and recommended she be sent to a nursing home for proper care and treatment. Thankfully, they found one that was just in the next town over; Tracy gets lifts from Jim or takes the bus and visits her mother three to four times a week. Sometimes, she doesn't recognize her straight away, and other days, she seems distant and sad, but the nurses are convinced that she's responding well to treatment and only needs time.

Jim finally broke the silence to speak to Tracy.

"What's going through your mind?" asked Jim.

"I've just been thinking….about a lot of things," said Tracy.

"Such as?" asked Jim.

"Such as my dad….if he'd been here, I don't believe that he would have done half of the things you did for me. He wouldn't have gone out of his way and risked his life to save me," said Tracy.

"I just did what I could", said Jim.

"But that's the thing, you do so much for me, Jim. We're not even related, and yet, whenever I need a shoulder to cry on or help with something, you're always there for me; even if I shut you down, you're still there," said Tracy.

"I'm always there when you need me; I'm your uncle, remember," said Jim.

"But that's just it….all the things you do…you're not my uncle Jim….you're my dad, the one I wish mine was," said Tracy with tears in her eyes.

Jim was feeling the same as he approached Tracy.

"And you're the daughter I wish I could have had", said Jim, also with tears in his eyes.

Both of them hugged each other rather emotionally. Then they stopped and dried themselves off.

"Okay, the emotional moment passed," said Tracy.

"Yeah," said Jim.

"So, what do you intend to do with yourself?" asked Jim.

"I don't know. I could've gone to college when I finished school, but with that photographer business and my dad leaving, I've had to look after my mom. I've only just been getting by on part-time jobs and the occasional education from you," said Tracy.

"I called up the New York College, the one that Derek planned to go to. I informed them about his death, and they got me talking about what I wanted to do. Then they said they could keep the spot open for me to join next year if I want it," said Tracy.

"And what did you say?" asked Jim.

"I said I'd think about it. They said they could keep it open until the end of this year, but if I don't give them an answer by then, they'll have to give it to someone else," said Tracy.

"Well, whatever you decide, Tracy, you know that I'll be there to support you," said Jim.

"Not in New York, though," said Tracy.

"Not there, right here," said Jim as he touched Tracy's heart.

"Damn, that's cheesy," said Tracy with a laugh.

"I know, but what can you do?" said Jim, also with a laugh.

"Come on, it's lunchtime, and I'm buying," said Jim as he led Tracy out of the cemetery.

"You know Jim, since I still have some free time on my hands, I was wondering something," said Tracy.

"What's that?" asked Jim.

"I was wondering if maybe I could come and work with you for a bit," said Tracy as Jim stopped walking.

"You want to work with me?" asked Jim.

"Well, I've got experience thanks to your teachings, and don't all private investigators need a beautiful and glamorous assistant to catch the criminals off guard and make them sing like a canary?" said Tracy.

"I knew showing you too much Private Eyes would go to your head," said Jim as Tracy laughed.

"Well, why don't we discuss our partnership over some of Rose's shepherd's pie," said Jim as Tracy happily smiled and walked towards the car.

Jim's phone suddenly rang.

"Wait by the car, Tracy, I'll be with you in a minute", said Jim as Tracy nodded, he answered the phone.

"Hey, Dylan," said Jim.

"Hey buddy, how's it been down there?" said Dylan.

"Recovering slowly, things are quiet and getting back to normal," said Jim.

"Glad to hear it...I...I attended the funerals of Francis and Fitzgerald last month; it was a good service. I had all the rifles, the flag and everything," said Dylan.

"Sorry I didn't come, it's just...." Jim couldn't finish.

"It's okay, Jim; I know you had your history with him. Anyway, the reason I called is because I have something really important to tell you," said Dylan.

"What is it?" asked Jim.

"We found him, Jim. We've found Alexi Sorkalov!" said Dylan.

"What, when?" asked Jim.

"Just yesterday, we managed to plant a CI in his organisation three months ago. He finally got Alexi out of hiding, and we had FBI agents waiting for him. He's been arrested along with a few dozen of his associates, his organisation has collapsed, and he's been charged to the full extent of the law," said Dylan.

Jim was bemused.

"Wow….well I….sorry Dylan, I'm just taken aback. I've spent the last five and a half years trying to help you guys find him, and now you have….well, at least he's done for, and maybe now, Matilda can rest in peace," said Jim.

"Yeah, you might want to hold off on that," said Dylan.

"What does that mean?" asked Jim.

"Alexi is being charged with a lot of stuff….except for Agent Sandra's murder," said Dylan.

"What?!" said Jim.

"He claims that it wasn't him who shot her; it was actually his second in command," said Dylan.

"Well, do you have him in custody?" asked Jim.

"No, he was arrested, but he broke free and escaped his transport while being taken to headquarters. But we have his name; he can't get far," said Dylan.

"What's his name, Dylan?" asked Jim.

"David Brandon," said Dylan.

The news hit Jim like a shot in the dark. For years, he believed that Alexi Sorkalov was responsible for Matilda's death. Now, he was not only being told that wasn't the case, but the man who killed her was the father of his best friend. Had Joey always known the man he was friends with had his chance of having a family robbed from him by his father, or was he completely oblivious to the fact?

"Thanks for that, Dylan," said Jim.

"No problem, man, I just wanted to let you know since….well, you're friends with a Joey Brandon, and according to the file, David is his father, so…." said Dylan.

"No, no, I get it; thanks for letting me know. I'll talk to you soon, Dylan, keep it real; bye," said Jim as he ended the call. Tracy came back over to him.

"Jim, is everything okay?" asked Tracy.

Jim was quiet for a moment; he didn't know what to say.

"I'm good, all good, Tracy; just a quick update from Dylan about how the funerals went. Now come on, before they run out of Shepard's pie," said Jim as he walked Tracy back to the car; they both got in and drove away.

The case was over, and everything seemed to be returning to normal in Milford. But will Jim attempt to follow up on Matilda's real killer? Will he tell Joey what he knows about his father? Or will he leave it to the FBI and keep the life he has in Milford intact?

That is a story for another time.

The End

Printed in Great Britain
by Amazon